DARK

MAGIC

DARK MAGIC

DARKHAVEN SAGA: BOOK TWO

DANIELLE ROSE

WATERHOUSE PRESS

ISBN: 978-1-64263-167-8

For Mom—
for believing in me, for supporting me,
and for being a better mom than Tatiana.
This one is for you.

ONE

There's something about the scent of blood from the undead. Its stagnant odor doesn't compare to the sweet aroma of the innocent. A girl could lose her mind thinking about the hot, crimson liquid coursing through a human's veins. I surrender myself to that very thought, even though I'm not actually feeding.

Even now, the scent of blood lingers in the air. It forms a heavy mist, coating my lungs with its tantalizing fragrance. It may not smell as lovely as human blood, but I react nonetheless. Instincts take over, and my stomach squeezes tightly in response. Pain flashes through me like a dagger to the gut. It feels like I haven't eaten in weeks, and even though I tell myself that's not true, my innards don't believe me. The pain never lessens. Instead, it permeates through me, like the spread of lightning on a hot summer day. It crawls across my skin, fanning like a sticky spider web.

When I was mortal, cannibalism—let alone self-cannibalism—never crossed my mind as something I'd be willing to try, but as I clutch my wounded arm to my chest, I fight the urge to relish in my own blood. I'm fairly certain feeding on myself won't sustain me, but the desire to lick my own arm clean doesn't wane.

The air is heavy in my lungs. Each inhalation stings

1

painfully, and I'm reminded that even the undead can die for good.

My breath comes in short, shallow huffs. I try to remain still, to calm my racing heart, but my chest burns from hunger. The pain has reached my heart, and with each passing second, the desire to feed overpowers my need to protect myself.

I know if I keep up this way of thinking, I won't survive the night.

My legs ache from running, so I rest against the trunk of a nearby tree. I'm surrounded by forest, the uninhabited land that cocoons the small town of Darkhaven—but I'm not alone.

My head is spinning, and I suspect it's from blood loss. I inspect my injury. Blood is smeared across my arm in thick slashes. I was careless. My attacker didn't have a weapon; I did. I was cocky, an all-too-confident amateur among experts. I didn't account for the force behind his vicious fists. There are five perfect streaks from where I raised my arms in defense to block his attack.

I wince when my fingers come into contact with tissue that was never meant to be bared. I curse inwardly as a rush of pain surges through me. It shouldn't take long to heal—one of the perks of being a vampire. Unfortunately, my strength is dwindling. The more energy I use to heal, the weaker I become.

I need to make a decision quickly. Am I the predator or the prey?

I settle on the ground, pulling my knees to my chest as I listen to my surroundings. Somewhere out there, there are at least a half dozen rogue vampires. I know *he* sent them. He's the monster that haunts my dreams. He's the reason I'll never see my eighteenth birthday as a mortal. He's the reason I was forsaken by the witches and left to fend for myself among the vampires.

I hate him with every fiber of my being, and I know he's watching, waiting for the perfect time to strike. He won't stop until he's claimed my soul—but I plan to take his first.

I'm annoyed by both his perseverance and cowardice. Instead of facing me himself, he sent his lackeys to do his dirty work. Each one is becoming more brazen than the next. This time, they caught Jasik and me off guard and smartly separated us.

Somewhere in these woods too far from home, where allies await our return, Jasik, my sire, is fighting for his life—and it's all because I wasn't strong enough to finish off my assailant the first time we met in that cemetery over a month ago. I grind my teeth at the thought of our initial meeting.

I was wounded and exhausted from a fight and from protecting Liv, my childhood best friend who was an inexperienced warrior. I had the audacity to feel grateful when he willingly left without a fight. After all, I wasn't sure I was strong enough to fight off another vampire, but I should have tried. I might have won, and I wouldn't be in the predicament I'm in now.

I used to think I wasn't a novice warrior, but letting my enemy escape was a rookie mistake—one I'm still paying for. I have a sneaking suspicion I will be paying for this mistake for the rest of my life.

The sound of twigs snapping under weight reaches my ears. I stop mentally berating myself for past mistakes and jolt upright. My arm isn't fully healed yet, but with each passing second, revitalized flesh threads together. Braided muscles intertwine with the old to make me stronger, faster, better. Soon, it'll look as if I was never wounded to begin with. I may not be shipshape yet, but this will have to do. I can't keep hiding in the brush, praying I'm not found. I'm no coward, and I won't let Jasik die fighting my battles.

I make eye contact with those who approach. Their crimson irises burn into mine. If looks could actually kill, I'd erupt into flames right about now. I can only hope the death daggers I'm throwing back are just as menacing.

The rogue vampires whistle as they make their way toward me. I step away from the tree and swallow hard. I clench my jaw shut and stand straighter, stronger. I'm outnumbered, but I've been training to fight vampires my whole life. I protected Darkhaven and my former witch coven from these evil creatures long before I became one myself. The only difference now is I can match their strength, their speed, their ferocity. I'm no ordinary witch anymore. I'm a witch-turned-vampire, and there's no wrath greater than that of a witch scorned.

I'm running before I've even decided to be the first to attack. It's as if my limbs have minds of their own. My attacks are instinctual and predatory. I race toward danger with the effortless ease of a lion hunting a gazelle. Unlike the lion, I have no intention of feeding on these beasts, but I will introduce them to the darkness that awaits after my stake plunges into their hearts.

The rogue vampires lunge toward me, and just before we make contact, I pounce into the air, striking both attackers in the chin with my feet. I kick up my legs with such force, I flip backward, landing several yards from the vampires. As my prey crawls to their feet, I withdraw my stake. It takes mere seconds for me to plunge it into the chest of one of the vampires. His eyes nearly bulge from their sockets before his entire body combusts into ash. The wind carries his remains away while I turn to face my final victim.

His fist meets my jaw with a hard snap. The crunch of bone rocks me to my core, and I stumble backward. I fall against a tree and cradle my chin in my hand. Blood spews from a laceration to my gums, and I greedily suck it down. Smiling, the rogue vampire licks his lips before charging toward me.

I glance around for my stake, finding it several paces in front of me. I know I'll never reach it in time.

I dig my fingers into the soil and wait until the vampire is in perfect range. As soon as he is, I kick my legs forward, thrashing at his chest. I plant a solid foot against his breastbone, and the vampire stumbles backward, falling to the ground in a reckless heap.

I jump forward, careful not to move my jaw as my bone mends. I plop onto the vampire's torso rather clumsily and dodge several of his weak attempts to remove me. I slam my legs together—once, twice, three times—and the vampire howls beneath me. I hear the echo of a rib cracking against pressure, and I have to fight the urge to smile—mainly because my jaw is technically still broken.

Just as I'm about to land a kill punch to the throat—one that will *surely* decapitate him—I see the flash of dark silver in the corner of my eye. I turn in time for the vampire to thrust my stake toward me. I didn't notice him scratching at the ground in his attempt to recover my weapon; I was too busy dodging his assaults. Suddenly, I understand why his punches were so shoddy. He was distracting me long enough to grab my stake.

The flash of metal is charging toward me, piercing the air as it nearly plunges into my chest. I grab on to the vampire's wrists and try to hold him back. But he's stronger than I am. For every centimeter I'm able to push him backward, he pushes forward two more. Soon, the tip that's graced so many vampire hearts is dangerously close to my own. The magic-infused silver tears through my jacket, and then my shirt, and soon, it's teasing the soft skin of my chest.

Once again, I smell my own blood as it wafts into the air around us. I cry out as the metal digs deeper into my flesh. My arms are weak, my jaw aches, and my heart is heavy. I don't want to say it—to even *think* it—but I fear I may not survive this battle.

Unable to hold on much longer, I slam my forehead against the vampire's. He winces on impact but doesn't falter. I hit him again and again, and just when I'm certain I can't hold him off any longer, his grip loosens.

I thrust my arms upward, forcing his apart. I hear the distinct sound of my stake falling to the ground as I smack my palm upward. I slam against the vampire's jaw with such force, his head is thrown backward. His arms slump beside him before his body dissolves into ash.

With the vampire dusted beneath me, I slouch forward, chest heaving. I wrap my fingers around the familiar cool metal of my stake and scan my surroundings. I know these two vampires aren't the only rogues stalking the forest tonight. If I'm not careful, I really may meet an untimely fate.

I sheath my stake in my jacket's inner breast pocket just as the night silence is pierced by a shriek. The deep timbre of this particular voice is one I will never forget. I know it well, but I've never heard such agony, such fear, come from it.

Jasik is in trouble.

Without thinking or fearing for my own life, I dash through the forest, running toward each wail and praying my sire will survive the torture the rogues are inflicting.

With each step, the sound of his pain grows louder, and

my ears ring from the noise. I worry I won't make it in time, but I cast those dark thoughts from my head and focus on my mission. I *will* save him.

I whip past fallen leaves and tear through brush, the crunch of dying foliage echoing through the forest. If the rogues thought I was dead, they certainly don't think that anymore.

Memories of a similar chase spring to mind, and my vision clouds momentarily. By the time I blink away the flashback, I almost collide with a tree trunk and am nearly decapitated by a low-hanging branch. I tumble forward, falling to my knees and skidding across the harsh landscape. The rough scrape of rocks against my shins sends shock waves through my body.

Clumsily, I stand, legs wobbling as I regain my composure. I brush off my hands and come to a screeching halt.

The remaining rogues surround Jasik. Blood pours from his mouth, seeping down his chin and splattering onto the ground. He lies still momentarily before struggling to stand. Finally, he withdraws his weapon, hand gripping the wrapped-leather handle of his blade. He spins in circles, waiting for the first attacks. I can't deny how eerily similar this resembles a witch circle. I shake away the feeling and ready myself to assist my sire. I just need to get Jasik's attention first.

As if our sire bond really did grant him psychic awareness, Jasik makes eye contact with me at the exact moment the rogues anticipate my arrival. We are severely outnumbered. I know there is no way we will survive this attack without help.

Something is said silently between us—a mutual understanding of our devastating predicament. We're both too stubborn to run for the hills, and we're both too smart to know that we'd never outrun a dozen rogues anyway. I nod in understanding.

Before I can make my move, the rogues are breaking away from Jasik and running toward me. I gasp, jaw slack with fear, and watch as they trample over the very brush I couldn't weave through without falling on my butt. I manage to tear my gaze from the sight before me and meet Jasik's eyes. He too is shocked by this turn of events. It's clear the rogues were never after *him*. They wanted *me*. Of course, I didn't need confirmation. I know who sent them, but now, Jasik does too.

I have maybe five seconds to save myself. The moment they're within reaching distance, I'm done. It will be over. I could barely handle myself against two rogues. I will never survive a dozen at once. Whoever decided rogue vampires are naturally more ferocious and stronger than regular vampires can suck it. Hard.

I'm shaking. I squeeze my palms, balling my hands into fists at my sides. My arms dangle, and my limbs become heavy. Fear erupts within me, threatening to consume every crevice of this immortal coil. I fight back the urge to . . . what? I can't explain what I'm feeling. I don't want to cry or run or scream. I don't want to die. In fact, I crave bloodshed in ways I never dreamed possible. But this bloodshed is never mine.

I tease the growing sensation that's forming in the pit of my gut. With each tantalizing internal caress, this urge strengthens.

My chest heaves, my breathing becoming erratic and loud. I clench my jaw shut, and all I can hear is each staggering breath echoing in my mind.

My heart is racing, my skin slick with sweat. Suddenly, I realize how unbearably hot it's become. The air around me is hazy, and when the mist lands on my skin, it sizzles and burns upon impact.

My arms are extended beside me, but I don't remember raising them. I'm shaking so badly now, I can barely stand straight. My knees buckle as I wobble from side to side, desperately trying to maintain my hold on . . . on whatever it is I have within my grasp.

I don't understand what's going on, but something within me is screaming at me not to stop. It's begging me to trust this alien presence, to succumb to it. I'm overwhelmed with the startling realization that this *thing* is our only chance at salvation. I came here to save Jasik, but instead, I will save myself. I have never played the role of damsel in distress, and I don't plan to start now. I *am* a savior.

The acidic heat is boiling within me, and I know it won't be long before the volcanic eruption wipes out everything within this forest. The second I try to warn Jasik with my eyes, I know it's already too late.

A brutal gasp of air is ripped from my lungs, and I wail louder, stronger, more fiercely than I ever believed possible. The sound leaving my lips sounds nothing like me. It's filled with such anger, such hatred, such *power*.

With each second I expel this foreign substance from the depths of my soul, a blast of heat permeates from my hands, my arms, my mouth. I struggle to control the blazing inferno that's seeping from my body.

The rogue vampires scream as the flames lick their skin, quickly turning each to ash. As soon as the final rogue embarks on his journey straight to hell, the power within me recoils. The flames retreat from the forest around me, dancing across the shadows until I swallow them whole.

I fall to my knees, weakened. Chest heaving, I run the back of my hand across my slick forehead and tumble over, but

Jasik is there to catch me. He lifts me gently, cradling my body in his arms. He wipes away the hair that's clinging to my skin and whispers that I'm okay, that *we're* okay.

I'm not sure how much time passes, but when I'm finally strong enough to stand on my own, Jasik releases me without objection. I claw at my chest, bunching the fabric of my jacket and T-shirt until I feel the strong, steady beat of my heart. I replay what happened over and over again, but each recollection of the events offers no greater explanation as to what actually happened.

"Ava?" Jasik speaks cautiously.

I nod in response but don't look at him. I'm still reeling from the events that just transpired.

"What was that?" he asks.

I swallow the knot that's formed in my throat and turn to face him. When I finally respond, my voice is but a whisper.

"Magic."

TWO

We are returning home in silence. Having just killed more than a dozen rogue vampires, we should be rejoicing. Our spirits should be high. There should be a party, with spiked blood and dancing under the stars while bathed in moonlight. Perhaps we'd even be skin-clad, and I would thank the moon for another night of eternal life. And once the party draws to an end, I should be looking for Malik, Jasik's brother, to discuss battle plans. Our training should continue as scheduled after I report the death toll to Amicia.

I should be doing all of these things. But I won't. None of that will happen tonight.

What transpired replays on a never-ending loop in my mind. I don't make eye contact with Jasik as we trudge closer to home, but I'm certain he's just as worried as I am. I crave peace and answers and solace. I'm sure he does too.

I'm a *vampire*. I relinquished my control over magic the moment I drank Jasik's blood. I exchanged light for dark, food for blood, mortality for immortality, and time for eternity.

But I was born a witch, and I *know* magic. Everything inside me is convincing me that the energy I harnessed to eliminate the rogue vampires is rooted in magic, but that can't be true. Has there ever been a vampire who could access magic? Is it even possible? What would that make me?

Such a creature certainly wouldn't be labeled something as simple as *vampire*. Today's events make me . . . *something more*. Something *better*. Something to bridge the gap between vampires and witches. I've given up hope that I'll ever be able to return home, but maybe this changes things.

I've never heard of a mixed creature, one that can access the characteristics of both species. Of course, Hollywood has, but this isn't a movie. This is the real world, and until I figure out what happened and learn to harness that energy for good, I am risking the lives of everyone around me.

After being forsaken by my former witch coven and offered refuge by the vampires, I can't bring them harm. If it weren't for them, I would have succumbed to my blood lust weeks ago, and I would have become one of the rogue vampires we hunt at night.

It's been six weeks since rogues attacked my coven.

It's been six weeks since I was murdered and brought back to life by Jasik. He sired me and risked his own neck in the process. I won't be the reason he risks his life *again*.

I kick at the sticks by my feet as we walk and grumble under my breath. It's frustrating that just as I was finally getting used to being a vampire and falling into my new life with the undead, something as potentially earth-shattering as *this* happens. I'm tired of lacking control, of being too weak.

The trees open to a small clearing. The brush has been compacted into the earth after far too many years of regular foot traffic. The soil beneath my foot transforms into hard stone, and I navigate the cobbled pathway with conditioned ease.

As I approach the short black wrought-iron fence that surrounds our home, I keep my gaze focused on the seemingly endless row of tiny crosses that tops each iron. The sharp slabs of metal bring all-too-familiar emotions, and I think of the silver cross necklace *Papá* gave me before he was killed by rogue vampires so many years ago. It's all I have left of my heritage, and I can't touch it. I can't embrace the cool metal and cry myself to sleep at night when the world is too hard and I just miss my family.

The moment I pass the threshold and can no longer stare at the crosses without craning my neck, I feel at ease. There's something about being home, knowing I'm safe and understanding any rogues who venture this far into the woods won't be escaping with their heads intact. The fear and confusion from earlier stops clouding my mind. I'm still worried about what this means, but I'm not as fearful of the answers. I glance at Jasik and know we will figure it out together.

Before me, the timeless Victorian manor we call home is three stories tall, with startling overhangs, sharp edges, and stained-glass windows. Jeremiah is settled on the wraparound front porch, and I pat one of the entry gargoyles on the head like I would greet a dog as I approach him.

The front stairs lead to French-style double doors, but I bypass the entry and beeline straight for Jeremiah's side. I plop down beside him and watch as he sharpens the blade of his weapon. Every time he swipes the metal sharpener across the length of the dagger, an ear-piercing crunching noise echoes in my mind. I shiver internally and try to break the silence by distracting myself with the view. Jeremiah has always been a man of few words, so I don't bother striking up a conversation.

I stare out at the dying grass lawn, careful not to make eye contact with Jasik, who has followed me over to where I now sit. In the distance, I hear the crashing waves against a wall of rocks. Darkhaven is bordered by the forest on three sides and the sea on another. We're lucky to be close enough to listen as the water comes alive. I inhale deeply and smell the air, which is heavy with mist. I may have been born a spirit witch, but I certainly favor the water element. Something about being near water makes me feel awakened, rejuvenated, alive.

A fog rolls over the land, slowly creeping upon us. It will reach us before we go inside. Something about it, about this night in particular, is too ominous for my comfort. All that's missing is an old cemetery and an eerie keeper of graves. As I watch the fog's slow but steadfast approach, I can't help but feel a pang of dread. It envelops my happy-go-lucky self and mocks my earlier comfort. Even though I'm trying to stay positive, I'm not naïve to the fact that a heavy threat hangs over me like the salty thick air that stings my lungs with each inhalation.

When I was just a witch fighting for my cause, back before I met Jasik and the vampires who now trust me with their lives, I knew something was going to happen. I was a spirit witch, which meant my powers were rooted in my psyche. I foresaw a horrific act, but I didn't know spirit was warning me of my own demise.

I had no idea I was going to die during our full moon ritual, but I knew danger was coming to Darkhaven, the place I've called home since birth. Sadly, no one believed me. Mamá brushed off my concerns and called me a novice spirit user. In the end, her inability to believe I could foresee something she couldn't cost me my life.

Tonight, I feel those very same warnings deep within my soul. As I watch the fog spread closer and closer, something aches within me. I feel restless, uneasy, and completely alert.

I fear something new, something *dark*, has come to Darkhaven, and it craves my life. This dark magic within my very being may be our only answer.

Jeremiah scrapes his blade against the sharpening rock and looks up at me. He furrows his brow, a look of confusion piercing his usually pristine face.

"Everything okay?" he asks. His dark skin is ashen in the moonlight, and I remind myself to search for the herbs I need for his skin elixir. I may not be a practicing witch anymore, but I can make one heck of a cream for his dry skin. I plan to surprise him with it, which is why I keep forgetting to gather the necessary ingredients. There aren't too many days when I'm left alone long enough to gather herbs and create an elixir.

Even now, Jasik is with me, keeping watch over the land … and me. Usually I don't mind, but today I wonder if it's because of what happened earlier. Is he worried I'll lash out and his friends will combust?

I'm distracted by the vampires who've just exited the manor and are making their way toward me. When they approach, the man gives me a sharp nod. They continue walking past until they disappear around the corner.

The front porch wraps around the length of the side of the house and ends at a hanging swing. I'm sure that's where they plan to rest until daybreak, when we're all cast back into the shadows until the moon graces us once again.

I've been here for six weeks, and I feel no closer to making any real friends. I know this has a little to do with my witchy upbringing, but it's mainly because Jasik broke the rules when he changed me.

Vampires aren't solitary creatures. They tend to live in nests with other vampires who have all been sired by the same vampire. In our case, that vampire is Amicia. I liken her to the high priestess of this vampire coven—if we can even be called that. I'm the only vampire living here she hasn't sired. Unfortunately, that means when I arrived, a target was on my back.

Slowly, over the past few weeks, Amicia has started to accept that I'm not going anywhere and have no intention of endangering her vampires, so it's about time her vampires welcome me too. The only friends I've made are the other hunters—Jasik, his brother Malik, Jeremiah, and Hikari. Together, we protect Amicia's vampires and kill rogues, who endanger everyone. Rogues are careless and kill without remorse. Sure, we survive on human blood too, but we're smart. Our existence goes unnoticed. Rogues would kill someone in a crowded room in broad daylight just for the heck of it if they could. If we don't stop them, humans will discover our existence, and life would become much harder for us.

Jeremiah clears his throat, breaking my concentration. I realize he has been staring at me. His crimson eyes glow beside his black skin.

"Hmm?" I ask.

"You okay?"

I nod, wondering how much information I should share. I glance at Jasik, who is stiff beside me, and I make the mental declaration that it needs to be Jasik who shares the events of today. Maybe if this revelation comes from him, as an onlooker to the massacre, it won't sound like I've been secretly planning something awful the whole time. Maybe they'll actually believe me when I tell them this was news to me too.

"Jer, gather the hunters, Amicia," Jasik says, breaking the silence.

Jeremiah arches a brow. "The hunt was that bad, huh?"

"There were . . . complications," I admit.

Jeremiah sits straighter. His interest has definitely piqued, but I'm not sure how much I should say without Amicia present. I'm sure she'll be annoyed if she's not at least present the first time I explain the magic outburst, and the last thing I need is to anger the only person keeping a roof over my head when the sun is up.

"What kind of complications?" Jeremiah asks, urging us to continue.

"Wait until we get inside," Jasik says.

He scans our surroundings, and I follow his gaze. I see nothing but darkness and a quiet forest. The fog is almost upon us now. Suddenly, I'm overwhelmed with the urge to get inside the manor. We're careful on our hunts. We track rogues quietly and attack at the perfect moment, but when we return home, we're far less concerned with onlookers or stalkers.

What if someone followed us home?

Someone could be watching us *right now*. They could easily be hiding behind a tree or within the fog. They may overhear what happened and spread the news of a vampire with access to witch magic.

They may have seen me in the woods.

"But you're both okay?" Jeremiah asks, still pressing for answers.

"Tell everyone we convene in five minutes," Jasik replies. This time, he's more forceful. His tone is harsh, abrupt, and Jeremiah gets the message. He nods sharply. He saunters inside, weapon and metal sharpener in hand, and disappears into the darkness, leaving Jasik and me to our thoughts.

I consider his question. *Are* we okay? I don't even

understand the definition of *okay* at this point. I'm not even sure if I'm okay, let alone if Jasik and I will find a way through this. After all, I nearly killed him too. If I'd held on to that magic even a second longer, the fire might have spread far enough to ... I shake my head. I can't think this way. We survived. That's all that matters.

Unfortunately, when I'm not worrying about my relationship with my sire or fearing Amicia's reaction to tonight's events, I'm thinking about one dreadful thing.

"I'm scared to tell her," I whisper to Jasik. I lean against him, finding comfort in his proximity. I glance down. The fog has spread through the air and coats the space around us in a thick white haze.

He shakes his head, brow furrowed. "Not here." He pulls away from me, and I feel empty without him near.

He places his index finger to his lips to silence my protest and points to the house and then to his ears. The vampires inside should have no issue eavesdropping. Their senses are just as heightened as ours. Of course, I know this, but I don't care.

"But if she thinks I'm a threat..." I stop speaking. Not because Jasik is pleading with his eyes for me to be quiet but because I can't say the words aloud. If Amicia thinks I'm too risky to have around, she'll cast me out. She made that promise the first night I arrived. The last thing I need is to be forsaken by *two* families.

It turns out, our gathering space for meetings—also known as Amicia's office—is just her bedroom with a corner desk. I'm uncomfortable invading her personal space, especially since we're sharing upsetting news. My arms dangle at my sides, and I scratch my nails against my palms. Malik eyes me curiously, so I unclench my fists and try to put off less strenuous vibes.

I glance around Amicia's room, trying not to look as nosy as I feel. Everything is bathed in purple. Her hardwood floors are stained dark, and the walls are the color of jam. Her bedspread is stitched with a deep-wine thread, with the pillars of the frame extending almost to the ceiling. A sheer, lacy canopy encloses the bed, but it too is a shade of purple. I'm surprised the space doesn't have an overwhelming feeling. The purple theme is a bit excessive for my taste, but the room has been attractively decorated.

Amicia clears her throat in a pointed manner. She's tired of waiting, Jasik is stalling, and I'm just snooping at this point. I glance at Jasik, noticing the crease around his eyes. He's nervous. Or perhaps he's trying to find the right words to explain what even I can't. I consider how I'd reveal today's events.

Amicia, I used magic.

Maybe I shouldn't admit to anything. The last thing I want her to believe is that I planned this all along. After all, we were once mortal enemies.

Amicia, is it possible for a vampire to access witch magic?

Maybe I shouldn't phrase it so pointedly. That's basically a confession.

Amicia, have you ever heard of a mixed creature?

That might be too vague.

I groan internally and focus on our tireless leader. Her black hair is shiny and sleek. It's slicked back and doesn't move even when she does. Her ebony skin is soft against the harsh shine of her leather attire. Her crimson irises are focused solely on me. I'm sure she knows the reason behind this unscheduled meeting has something to do with the hunt tonight, which I was part of.

I swallow hard and offer a bleak smile. I mumble incoherently and make some sort of soft snort. Everyone in the room is staring at me now, and I just want to die. There's something about Amicia that makes me want to confess my sins and offer my life to her. Jasik explained it's because of her age. The older the vampire, the more powerful the vampire. Amicia is the oldest vampire I've ever encountered, and I whimper under her stare. It's really annoying, actually. She has a mysterious power over newborn vampires—and those she sires—and I hate that feeling of attachment. I'm not good at losing control.

"Someone speak," Amicia says plainly. She emphasizes each word, and a combined shiver courses through the room. It's as if we all felt that order.

I inhale dramatically, preparing myself to admit my faults and pack my bags. Thankfully, I'm not given the chance.

"Something happened on our hunt tonight," Jasik says, saving me from my inevitable damning confession.

"I assumed as much. Stop stalling," Amicia says. She waits for Jasik to continue.

"We were ambushed. There had to be nearly two dozen rogue vampires," he says.

Hikari gasps and Malik frowns. I've been training with Malik for six weeks now. I know that look. He's replaying battle plans in his mind, trying to find one that explains how we survived. I'm confident he won't figure it out.

"That many? So close to home?" Amicia asks. Her voice

is laced with her concern, but her face doesn't betray her fear. I suppose time has helped her perfect her poker face.

Jasik nods and crosses his arms. His T-shirt strains against his muscles. "We stayed in the woods, not even venturing into town. They were waiting for us."

"Why?" Amicia asks.

"Because of her," Jasik responds, looking at me. The others follow suit, and I whimper under their stares. I'm also not good at being the center of everyone's attention. I've always preferred the solace I've found in the night. It's as if I was created to become a vampire.

"What do they want with you?" This time, Amicia is speaking to me, not Jasik.

I exhale slowly, preparing myself for my confession and silently wondering how much information she cares to know. I decide to tell her everything.

"Just before the full moon ritual, I went patrolling with Liv, a friend from another coven. We survived, but I was weakened. I didn't see that there was another vampire hiding, watching. He cornered us, and I knew I wasn't strong enough to fight him off too. Liv was new to patrolling, and I wasn't sure if she was strong enough to battle him alone."

I glance at Jasik, who nods. That's the confirmation I need to continue. It occurs to me that I've never told him this story either.

"In the end, this vampire left without a fight, but he threatened he'd be back. I brushed it off. That wasn't the first time I'd been threatened by a vampire. Sometimes they did come back, but I was always prepared."

Instinctively, I reach for my stake. I run my hand over the cool silver. The other vampires' gazes zone in on my movement.

They all know what's hidden there. I'm not sure how they feel about it, but already it's saved my life. As long as I'm hunting rogues, I'll never relinquish my favored weapon.

"This is the vampire who attacked my coven at the full moon ritual. He was the one who bit me just before you saved me."

I'm looking at Jasik, who furrows his brow, no doubt trying to replay his recollection of that night in his mind. I never knew what happened to that vampire after Jasik and his friends showed up. I was too busy dying to really see much. I know the vampire was taken by surprise, because I could see that in his eyes. I also know Jasik ripped him off me before he could complete his promise. Everything else has kind of faded away. I'm grateful I don't have many memories from that night. I see it in bits and pieces, and honestly, that's enough. It's bad enough that I remember their screams.

"This vampire was in the woods tonight?" Amicia asks.

"I'm not sure. I didn't see him, but . . . I *feel* him."

This time, Amicia gives me an astonished look. "What do you mean, you *feel* him?"

I shrug. "I think it's just the predator in me. It doesn't like being prey."

I glance at Malik, who is fighting a grin. He said that very line to me during one of our training sessions. I was being overly stubborn, and he had to knock me down a few notches so I would benefit from the session.

"I know he sent those rogues. He's testing me," I say.

"It seems like he wants you dead," Hikari interjects.

I nod. "He does. I'm sure he hopes he'll be the one to do it, but obviously he doesn't mind if one of his lackeys does it for him. If he cared, he wouldn't keep sending them to do his dirty work."

"That seems like a lot of trouble to go to just because of one grudge," Hikari argues.

"He's tried to kill me . . . what, four times now? He's failed every single time. This isn't a grudge. This is personal. He's challenged me, and I continuously best him. I'm a threat to his pride and leadership."

"He won't stop until one of you is dead," Jasik says.

"I know," I say.

"Well, we'll just have to make sure he's the one who ends up dust," Jeremiah says. He cracks his knuckles, and I smile.

"We can introduce more training sessions," Malik suggests.

I nearly choke on my breath. The last thing I want to do right now is fight Malik. I can't risk hurting him—or setting our house on fire.

"I'm not sure—" I begin but am interrupted by Amicia.

"You say there were nearly two dozen rogue vampires?"

Jasik nods. "That's correct."

"How did the two of you survive?" she asks. Her voice is void of emotion.

"At first, Ava and I worked together to eliminate a few, but then we were separated . . ." Jasik trails off.

"What happened then?" Amicia asks.

The room is silent for far too long. The echo of steady heartbeats—two of which are racing—bounces around my mind. I know this is it. Jasik is waiting for me to explain what he doesn't understand.

"I fought off two attackers, and then I heard Jasik scream. By the time I reached him, he was surrounded by rogues. We were both injured, and I knew we couldn't outrun that many vampires."

Amicia nods, waiting for me to continue.

"Something happened," I whisper.

"What happened?" I don't miss the annoyance in Amicia's tone. She's been asking us to get to the point of this meeting and her patience is dwindling.

"I used magic," I say. I may not understand what happened, but I'm confident magic was the source of that blast of energy.

The room erupts into shock. The gasps are so loud, I fear they may physically lash out at me. I wait for Amicia to respond, but she doesn't. Instead, her vampires express her confusion for her.

"What?" Jeremiah says.

"How is that possible?" Hikari asks.

"I don't know," I say.

"Amicia, you don't seem surprised," Jasik says.

I watch her. She seems lost in thought as she processes my words. My sire is right. She doesn't seem surprised. I may even be as bold as to say she was expecting this turn of events.

"You're the first witch-turned-vampire I've ever met, Ava. Your heritage makes you special," she says.

I want to thank her, but I don't. While I appreciate her words, I have a feeling her definition of *special* isn't the same as mine.

"What does this mean?" Jasik asks.

"What are you thinking?" Malik asks Amicia.

The two brothers speak in unison.

"I'm wondering if we should have anticipated this. Magic is inherently part of her. She was born this way, and perhaps even a vampire's bite and blood cannot change that part of her," Amicia says.

"But a *mixed* vampire? A...what? Hybrid creature? Is

that even possible?" Hikari asks.

Amicia doesn't respond. Instead, she closes the space between us and stands before me. She's so close, we're breathing the same air. I inhale each of her exhalations, and it's oddly arousing. Unfortunately, Amicia doesn't just radiate power. She permeates sex appeal too. I inhale deeply. She smells like coconut oil. The fragrance is delectable.

I do not break eye contact with her. I know she is not challenging me, but I can't look away. I can't submit to her dominance.

"Part vampire," she whispers.

"Part witch," I finish.

"I guess we should thank Jasik for saving her. If a half-breed is going to exist, we probably want her on our side," Jeremiah says.

Hikari elbows him in his gut, to which he feigns overdramatic discomfort before winking at her. Hikari rolls her eyes.

"Holland," Amicia says.

The room falls silent. Something is happening, and I break eye contact to glance at Jeremiah, who has paled so quickly, I'm actually concerned for his well-being. I almost ask if he's okay, but I don't bother. Everyone in the room is staring at him except for Amicia. She's still looking at me. Even though I've broken eye contact, I feel her gaze on me. Her crimson irises are burning holes into the side of my head.

"Is that really necessary?" Jasik asks.

"We need to understand what's happening here. Who better to ask than a witch?" Amicia asks.

"A witch?" I say, thoroughly confused. This time, I look at Amicia again. "Holland is a witch?"

She doesn't respond. She turns on her heel to face the others and orders Jeremiah to contact Holland.

"Explain I request his steadfast return home. I expect him at nightfall."

Jeremiah nods harshly before storming from the room. He doesn't close the bedroom door, and I hear him stomp down the hallway toward our living quarters.

Of course I'm concerned. I don't know what's going on, and so far, no one is itching to fill me in. But I don't worry about that now. I can only focus on Amicia's words.

Holland.

A witch.

Come *home*.

THREE

The next day, nightfall comes at an agonizing pace. The sun sets, the moon rises, and the mysterious Holland is still nowhere to be seen. I washed and dressed quickly because I didn't want to miss his arrival. Part of me is excited because Amicia seems to think he'll have answers, but mostly I'm crazy obsessed with the idea of being around a witch again. I barely slept last night, tossing and turning and watching the clock. I just about drove myself insane. I can still hear the slow, steady ticks of the second hand making its way around the clock face.

It's no surprise I'm the first one up. I'm still getting used to my new sleep schedule, so I'm almost always the first one awake. I can feel when the sun sets—and when it will soon rise. I suppose that's an essential perk of being a vampire, one who will literally burst into flames if I misread the clock hands and walk outside.

I inhale slowly and close my eyes, trying to ease my nerves. I'm so excited to meet Holland and spend time with someone who truly understands the witch in me, but at the same time, I'm terrified he won't have an answer to my problem. I'm not sure how long everyone will risk having me around. I guess that's why Amicia asked Holland, a witch, to come here. Desperate times call for desperate measures.

Trying not to think about my situation, I listen to the

manor. It's quiet, with only the creaks of an old house to keep me company. I know everyone will soon rise, and I'll miss this peace. But for now, I so desperately want it to be broken by the sound of the front door opening, signaling the arrival of Holland. Amicia says he's powerful, and she trusts him with this issue. I just hope he's experienced with my particular situation.

I exhale sharply and glance around the room. I'm sitting alone in the kitchen, slurping a mug of blood that's already cooled back to room temperature. I consider nuking it again, but the rush of incoming footsteps distracts me. Someone is awake. I'm giddy with excitement. If the house is waking, that means Holland should soon be here. I'm so excited I nearly clap with glee.

I'm sitting at a kitchen table, which is directly across from the cream-colored cabinets and steel appliances. From where I'm seated, I can easily keep my eye on the door to the kitchen. No one can enter from the dining room without alerting me. I'm offering a wide, toothy grin before Hikari has even walked into the room. When she sees me, she eyes me curiously but says nothing.

The swinging kitchen door closes behind her as she makes her way to the refrigerator. It offers me a few glances of the empty butler's pantry, which connects the kitchen to the dining room. From this, I discover Hikari is alone. Everyone else is probably slowly waking, but for now, we have privacy.

"You're up early," Hikari says. She yawns and stretches while cracking her back. Each crunch of her spine sends a shiver rushing through me.

I glance out the window and look into the backyard. I suppose it is early. The world is bathed in moonlight, and the stars sparkle and shine in the dark sky. I may still be adjusting to this new life, but I certainly can appreciate the darkness. I've always had an affinity for the moon. I turn back to face Hikari.

Shrugging, I opt for honesty when I say, "I guess I'm just—"

"Excited to meet Holland?" Hikari interrupts. She grins, her eyes brightening as if she's reading my mind. She crosses her arms over her chest and watches my reaction. She's giving me a knowing look, one that mimics the coy smiles boys would give their friend when the girl he likes enters the room.

"Is it that obvious?" I ask. I can't help the hiccupped giggle that escapes my lips. I feel like I'm a kid again and tomorrow is Yule morning. I'm excited to see what presents are in store for me.

She nods and laughs. "Totally obvious."

Holding back a smile, I watch her curiously. She's dressed in dark clothing, and her dagger is strapped to her waist. Her jet-black hair is tied back into a thick ponytail, and her skin, usually the color of warm ivory, is pale. I wonder if it's because she's hungry or because she's due to patrol the forest. After our meeting last night, it's no secret that rogues are targeting us. She shouldn't be patrolling alone.

I finger the coffee mug in front of me, spinning it round and round. It's full of blood, and a little splashes over the side, and I wipe it clean with a nearby napkin. When I'm done, I bunch the dirty napkin into a ball in my hand and let it roll away from me toward the center of the table.

"Excited is good, but you don't need to be nervous," Hikari says as she joins me at the table. She's holding her own mug of steaming blood. I lick my lips at the sight of it. Mine is still cold and murky. It lacks that extra *something*, that special life force that comes with that perfect temperature, the exact ninety-eight-point-six degrees. When it's too hot, it takes like burnt milk, and when it's too cold, it tastes like a melted Popsicle. When it's not the right temperature to maintain proper consistency, it just doesn't taste the same.

I glance at Hikari's mug one more time. We're drinking the same thing, but her breakfast looks so much better than mine. I glance back at mine and cringe. My stomach is queasy at the thought of finishing this as is, so I stand, walk to the microwave, and nuke my mug. While waiting, I face Hikari and lean against the counter, crossing my arms over my chest.

"I guess I'm just curious more than anything else. Amicia seems to think Holland has all the answers," I say.

Hikari snorts and rolls her eyes. "Don't get too excited. I'm not sure you should expect answers. Just... Don't go into today thinking he'll know what's going on, because you might be setting yourself up for a major disappointment." She slurps down a large swallow of blood, and my stomach grumbles.

"Why else would Amicia ask Holland to come here? He must know *something*," I say. More than anything, I want to ask Hikari *why* a witch is on a vampire's speed dial. I don't know all the details surrounding Holland's place in a vampire nest, and I know I'm not going to get answers from Jeremiah, Malik, or Jasik. Hikari is my only option. I just hope she's in a sharing mood.

There is a long pause while Hikari takes a sip of her blood. From the cross look on her face, she's considering my question and debating what she should share. Maybe the Holland situation is juicier than I originally thought.

"Before you, Holland was our only connection to the witches," she says. "It makes sense for Amicia to reach out to him for help. Your... *issue* is clearly magical. Who better to help than another witch?"

I nod, noting how she is trying to avoid actually answering my question. "So who is he?"

Hikari exhales slowly, loudly, as if she was hoping I wouldn't ask this. Thankfully, I don't have to wait long for her response. "He's Jeremiah's ex."

My eyes nearly bulge from their sockets. I'm not sure what I was expecting. After Jeremiah's reaction to Amicia's request to contact him, I assumed Holland left on bad terms, but I didn't realize the two had been romantically involved. No wonder Jeremiah was adamant about not inviting him over. After our impromptu meeting ended, I heard Jeremiah arguing with Jasik. He downright refused to be the one to reach out.

It doesn't take a spirit witch to foresee that things didn't end well between them, and I'm sure that's putting it mildly. In the end, Jasik convinced him to send Holland a text. As far as I know, Holland never replied, and now we're all waiting to see if he actually comes.

"I hope he shows up," I say. Suddenly, I'm overcome with worry. If things are still bad between Jeremiah and Holland, he might not come, and if he doesn't come, I'm out of options. Who else will help a witch-turned-vampire with way too much magical baggage? We have some pretty specific requests that only experienced witches can help with.

"He will," Hikari says. She speaks so matter-of-factly, my hopes actually rise. My heart flutters, and for a short time, I believe everything will be okay.

"How can you be so sure?" I ask. In my mind, I'm crossing my fingers that Hikari's response doesn't burden my lifted spirits.

"He owes us a favor," Hikari says, and my interest is

piqued. I arch a brow, silently begging Hikari to spill the beans. So far, she's told me more than I could get out of anyone else; why stop now?

"What kind of favor?" I ask, leading her. I've never been an instigator, but my life and safety may literally be on the line here. And I just plain want the details. For the first time in weeks, I feel like I'm just regular Ava—the one post-death—and I'm gossiping with my friend about the drama in Darkhaven. A rush of regret washes over me as I realize it's Hikari with me now, not Liv, my former best friend. Since she's a witch and I'm a vampire, our friendship was severed the moment I drank Jasik's blood.

"It's nothing interesting." Hikari shrugs. "Amicia saved his life once." She takes another long chug from her mug and then licks her lips as some blood drips down her chin. She wipes it away with the napkin ball I left at the table.

The microwave dings, and I nearly trip over my feet as I spin around to remove my mug. Carefully, watching the rim to avoid spilling, I return to the table with Hikari. Soon, the house will be alive with noise, and the room will be full of hungry, eavesdropping vampires. If I want information, I need to act quickly.

"And she's willing to cash in her favor for me?" I ask. Honestly, I'm not sure how that makes me feel. It's as if she actually does consider me part of her family. Have I *finally* proven myself to her? When I first arrived here with Jasik and the other hunters, Amicia made it clear that she's not giving me second chances. One mistake and I'm booted. I'd be lying if I said fear of being rejected by yet another family hasn't caused a few restless nights. I'm tired of looking over my shoulder and watching what I say. I don't want to walk on eggshells anymore.

It's exhausting.

Hikari dismisses me with the wave of her hand. "Knowing Holland, he'll call for another favor soon anyway. That's pretty much how our relationship has been with him. After we met, he moved in and ended up falling for Jeremiah. When things ended there, he left but kept the same phone number for 'emergency purposes.'" She uses air quotes to emphasize her words. "He's not fooling anyone. They aren't an item anymore, but he still cares for Jer. Sure, Holland said the number was for everyone, but I know the truth. They fell hard, fast, and those kinds of feelings don't just go away after one stupid fight."

"I suppose not," I say. I find it interesting that Holland was even able to live here. After all, he is a *witch*. He's not like me. He's still *alive*. The vampires here didn't take to me too well. I used to think that was because of my ancestry, but apparently they didn't mind Holland living here. I guess they're just nervous around me because Amicia isn't my sire. Wondering if Jasik and I will ever be forgiven for events that were completely out of our control, I exhale sharply and take a sip of my blood. I thought I would have fewer questions after learning about Holland, not more.

"Stop stressing," Hikari says, breaking through my thoughts. "Everything will be okay. Holland is a powerful witch. He'll know what to do."

"But that just makes me more confused. What powerful witch leaves his coven to live with vampires? He would be forsaken, like me. Living the rest of your days without family sounds awful," I argue.

Hikari shrugs and chugs the rest of her blood. She walks it to the counter. After rinsing it and leaving it in the sink for someone else to wash, she dries her hands on a nearby hand towel and turns to me.

"Look, I'm not going to uncover any dirty secrets Holland wants buried. If he wants to talk about his past or what happened with Jeremiah, he'll tell you himself. In the meantime, you need to focus on your own problems. And Ava, you have enough to keep your mind busy for a *long* time."

I snort, nodding, and finish the rest of my breakfast. When I'm done, I meet Hikari by the sink. Mindlessly, I consider her words while washing our mugs and setting them on the drying pad. I use the same hand towel to dry my own hands. I can feel Hikari's gaze on me, but I'm too preoccupied with my own thoughts to care about her watching me.

"Well, lovely chat, but I'm heading out to patrol, and I think you're due in the training room," Hikari says. She taps her wrist where a watch would sit if she actually wore one and offers a coy smile, at which I roll my eyes. I'm certain Malik has been waiting for me ever since I woke up, but I'm not ready to spar. I'm still shaky from yesterday, and I don't want to miss Holland's arrival.

I'm too preoccupied with my thoughts to realize Hikari is walking away. By the time I shout to her, she's already in the dining room and heading for the front door.

"Be careful tonight!" I yell.

❖

There's something about the feel of a weapon in my hand. The cool metal radiates power, sending shock waves from my hands into every nook of my body. Knowing I have the power to end life leaves me euphoric. I imagine this is why so many vampires choose to turn rogue, abandoning our practices and choosing death and power over secrecy and longevity.

I'd be lying if the thought of turning off my emotions and simply living by my urges didn't appeal to me. If that were possible, it would be so easy to walk away from everything I once knew, to stop fighting for the weak and live among the powerful. Of course, that's easier said than done. I can't literally turn off my emotions, and it seems far too great a hassle to simply pretend I don't have any at all.

An exasperated Malik exhales sharply. His usually unemotional face is pierced with his frustration. "Ava, please. *Focus.*"

Guilt gnaws at my innards. I offer a weak smile and say, "Sorry. I'm just ... distracted." I shrug.

"I understand your excitement, but training must remain your priority," Malik says.

I nod sharply. He doesn't need to remind me that this is important. I know it is. But the anticipation over the incoming Holland isn't my only distraction. I can't stop worrying about Hikari, who's hunting alone, and I'm afraid I'll let loose and unleash a magical blast that will bring down the entire house. The last thing I need on my conscience is leaving a dozen vampires homeless.

"This just isn't a good time," I say, defeated.

Malik furrows his brow as if he thinks I'm still not taking this seriously. I know he doesn't believe that I've made training with him a priority, but he should. I want to become stronger, faster, better. I don't want to fear for my life when I'm outnumbered by rogue vampires, who are our naturally more ferocious enemies. I want to aid my friends when they need me. I don't want to worry that the witches might come for their revenge, and I want to trust I can protect myself against the mysterious vampire who keeps sending his goons after me.

"Do you fear for my safety? Is that why you're holding back and not focused?" Malik asks.

"I, uh..." I shake my head. Of course I'm worried about that. I can't control myself when the heat of the moment overtakes my self-control.

"You don't need to worry about me, Ava. You can't hurt me," Malik says.

"You don't know that," I whisper. I wish he would take this seriously. He wasn't there when I engulfed our enemies in flames. I killed so many rogues with the mere snap of my fingertips. If Malik was smart, he'd never train with me again.

The basement training quarters provides the perfect sparring room. The mat floor is squishy, and except for one row of floor-to-ceiling mirrors and a section of displayed weapons, the walls are padded. It's like we're fighting inside a marshmallow. The cushion is just enough so we don't get injured, and since I spend most of my time falling on my butt down here, I can say that with confidence. I'm sure that's why Malik believes I can't hurt him. This room is designed to withstand a thrust to the chest, but it's not meant for a blast of magic. And even though Malik is trying to reassure me, he cannot survive a fireball to the face.

Malik walks toward me and rests a hand on my shoulder. I look up at him. He's smiling down at me. His eyes are soft, his gaze telling me everything will be okay. If only I could believe that...

"I—sorry, I'm just not ready for this yet," I say. "It's too dangerous, and I can't concentrate."

"Ava..." Malik's voice is calm, soft. In this moment,

he looks so much like Jasik, his younger brother, yet still so different. Malik is older, and the world-worn look in his eyes betrays that. He and his brother have survived far too many years of pain, torture, and solitude. They've experienced more death than any person should in one lifetime. I think that's why Malik is so closed off from his emotions. Rarely do I see him react to anything.

"It's not safe to spar. Not yet. Not until Holland..." I trail off. Not until Holland what? I'm not sure what Holland can do besides help me learn control. I'm guessing this foreign power inside me is here to stay. I just hope I can learn to control it so it doesn't control me.

"I said you *can't* hurt me," Malik says. "Not because you're unable to but because you have no desire to injure me. You *won't* hurt me, Ava."

"How can you be so sure?" I whisper. "You weren't there..."

"I don't need to witness your power to trust you have no yearning to use it against me," he says.

Malik drops his arm and takes a step toward me. I swallow the knot that forms as he closes in on me.

"Your power, your strength, is no different than mine. I'm strong. I'm the enemy of a witch, yet I feel no urge to protect myself around you. I never have."

Looking into each other's eyes, we breathe the same air. He reaches forward and brushes loose strands of my hair from my eyes and tucks it behind my ear. The way he looks at me, the way he touches me, is warm, familial. Malik is the brother I never knew I needed. When he looks at me, I can feel his devotion to protect his family. Slowly, we're becoming that to each other.

The day I died and was reborn, I would have given all that I own if only my former coven would take me back. Now, I can't imagine living without the vampires. It's hard to remember the girl I used to be. It's strange to think there was a time when Jasik wasn't my sire and Malik wasn't my trainer.

"You can't hurt me, Ava, so stop worrying that you will," Malik whispers. He offers a small smile before pulling away.

Someone clears her throat behind us, and we spin around to face the intruder.

"Hikari, you're back," Malik says. He takes several steps away from me and toward her.

I turn to see her frowning at me and gnaw on my lip. I breathe quickly, trying to steady my racing heart. I can't help but feel like a child who's just been caught stealing a cookie before supper. While I know our intentions were good and true, an onlooker might not be privy to that knowledge.

"How was your patrol?" I ask, hoping to steer our conversation in another direction. Even though I wish she would have caught us in the midst of an epic sparring session rather than staring deeply into each other's eyes, I'm grateful to see Hikari safe and unharmed. I truly was concerned for her well-being. Hunting alone when we have a target on our backs is just plain sloppy leadership.

"It was . . . strange," she says.

Strange? Kind of like walking in on Malik and me sharing an intimate moment and probably assuming it to be something it's not? I shake away the thought.

"How so?" Malik asks, clearly interested. I wonder if he was worried about her patrol too. Unlike me, he rarely showcases his emotions. I've seen more from him today than I've ever seen before.

"Well, I didn't run into any rogues, so I kept venturing farther and farther into the woods. Eventually, I ended up close to your old coven. I decided to check in on them—"

"You *what*?" I shout, interrupting her. "Why would you do that?"

"Well, I was nearby, and someone needs to keep an eye on them," she says.

"If they see you, they'll think we've been spying on them this whole time," I say.

"And they would be correct. I don't trust them, Ava! Someone needs to be watching them," Hikari shouts.

"Relax, both of you," Malik says. His voice is loud enough to tear through the tension-filled room. "What happened when you got there?"

"It looked like they were getting ready to go into the woods. They had stakes and crosses and were clearly dressed in combat clothes."

I furrow my brow. How's that possible? No one from my coven ever patrolled. I took control of that and never looked back. I was under the impression Mamá didn't really approve of my patrols, but she understood the importance of keeping the humans of Darkhaven safe.

"What is it, Ava?" Malik asks. I didn't realize the room fell silent, and the two of them were now staring at me.

"This doesn't make sense. They wouldn't patrol," I say.

"Who would take over for you?" Hikari asks.

I shake my head. "I don't know. No one, I guess."

"Well, if you want to talk about something not making sense…" Hikari trails off, and Malik clears his throat. She offers a weak apology and waits for me to continue.

"What exactly were they doing?" I ask.

"They were preparing to patrol. I know what that looks like, Ava." Hikari doesn't try to hide her annoyance.

"But then what?" I ask, urging her to continue.

She frowns. "It was weird. They entered the woods through the gate in your backyard, and then they all scattered. No two witches stayed together."

I meet her gaze, and something in my eyes must alert her.

"What is it?" Malik asks.

"My coven wasn't experienced in fighting, and they happily left it to me. But that doesn't mean they didn't teach everyone basic combat tactics. They were sure group attacks would be necessary one day," I say. I guess they were right. Without me, all they have is each other.

"So what does that mean?" Hikari asks.

"Think about it. When you're hunting in a group and close to your enemy, you break off individually to surround her."

Hikari gasps. I assume the realization is hitting her hard. Tonight, she risked her neck to patrol alone because the rest of us were too busy or too distracted to help. Then she checked in on the witches because no vampire in this house trusts them— unfortunately, that now includes me too.

"Hikari, they knew you were there. The witches were hunting you."

FOUR

The rush of excitement upstairs distracts me long enough to forget about the threat of the witches. Ever since I transitioned into a vampire, my senses became heightened. With a more acute sense of hearing, I'm able to home in on specific noises. The foyer is directly above us, and the distinct sound of muffled greetings sends me on edge. A visitor has arrived, and that can only mean one thing.

Holland is finally here.

Understanding we will need to discuss the witch debacle another time, Malik, Hikari, and I exit the basement sparring quarters and rush upstairs. I can barely contain my excitement. It's been far too long since I've had another witch to talk to, and I just may discover what happened during my transition. Clearly something went awry. I shouldn't be able to access magic, but for some reason I can. Now I just need to learn how to control it—that is, as long as this isn't some fluke that will pass.

Briefly, I let myself pretend this magic is here to stay *and* I can control it as well as I controlled it before I became a vampire. I envision a future where the alien energy source yields to me, and I wield it to do my bidding, not the other way around. Our nightly hunts would be so much easier.

The stairs to the basement lead to the kitchen, which is

at the back of the manor. Quickly I make my way through the kitchen and into the dining room. I ascend upon the sitting room and can see the swarm of vampires huddled in the foyer. Jasik is there.

As soon as I approach, my sire and I make eye contact. Something glistens behind his gaze, and I realize he too is excited for Holland's arrival. I suppose he wants answers as badly as I do. For the briefest of moments, I let myself believe he desires those answers because he cares for me—and not because it'll help the vampires of this household better understand our situation. He needs Amicia and the vampires to forgive him as much as I need them to fully accept me, not just *tolerate* me.

It's no secret there is a budding attraction growing between us. Even though I was raised to hate vampires, I feel as though I was born to become one. I've always preferred night to day, solitude to crowds, and even the liquid diet doesn't bother me much anymore.

As one of my former coven's only spirit users, I was always singled out. I never felt comfortable—even Mamá kept me at a distance after Papá died. When I was growing up, I thought that was because she secretly blamed me for his death. Instinctively, I reach for my cross necklace, only to find my neck bare.

If there's anything I need to get used to, it's not drinking blood, staying out all night, sleeping all day, and avoiding humans as if they're the plague; it's completely relinquishing my past life as if it never existed. I can never again find solace in what once comforted me.

I can't see Holland, but I know he's here. The swarm of vampires standing in the foyer is a dead giveaway. I scan their faces. Jeremiah is conveniently missing. I'm sure that's because of their bad breakup. I make a mental note to thank him later. Holland might not have shown up for anyone else.

The vampires clear, giving me full view of our intruder, and I don't give the Jeremiah-Holland situation another thought; I'm too focused on the witch before me.

Holland is tall, thin, pale-skinned, with floppy brown hair fluttering atop his head. As soon as the door closes and the breeze dies down, his hair settles into a heaping mess. I imagine he trekked quite the journey to get here in a day's time.

It occurs to me I know nothing about this man except for what Hikari told me—and that wasn't much. I don't know why he left his coven or where he lives now. I don't know the circumstances surrounding his first arrival here and his relationship with Jeremiah. I don't know if he's expecting a favor from me in return for his knowledge. In my entire life, I've never felt so unaware of my situation and surroundings. And that says a lot since I'm used to being both hunter *and* hunted.

The closer I walk toward Holland, the more I assess him. His chestnut eyes are soft, kind. When he smiles, there are wrinkles in the skin around his eyes, and there are dimples in his cheeks. He laughs at something one of the vampires says, and I relish in how comfortable he seems. It's as if he's not the only mortal in the midst of immortals. Nothing about him screams fear or hatred. In fact, he seems like he's finally come home.

He and I make eye contact, and I freeze. My breath catches in my throat, and I nearly choke on it. Someone collides with me from behind, and I feel the press of his solid body against my own. Malik wraps his hands over my arms and breathes against my head. He asks if I'm okay, but I don't answer. I'm unable to, and I can't seem to break eye contact with Holland.

Taking the initiative, our visitor walks toward me, a smile creasing his face. His features are delicate, and absolutely nothing about him is threatening. But I can't help the urge to run away, to fight, to survive. This is the first time I've been this close to a witch since my transition and acceptance into my new vampire lifestyle, and it's as if the vampire in me is warning me of impending danger. My natural instincts kick in—it's fight or flight.

Or is there another choice? Can there be something more? The vampires here have already shown me witches and vampires can be friendly. Everything I grew up believing isn't true. The witches lied, and now I can't shake the innate discomfort I feel when I'm around Holland. I pray it won't be this way forever.

To say I'm disappointed is an understatement. I had such high hopes for this meeting, for Holland's knowledge. I thought I'd have someone to share my witchy wisdom with. I thought we'd become friends.

"You must be Ava," Holland says. He walks toward me, stopping only an arm's reach away, and offers me his hand. "I'm Holland." He gives me a wide, genuine smile and waits for me to reciprocate.

My gaze drops to his hand, and I stare at it momentarily. I lick my lips and swallow the knot that has formed. Slowly, I reach for his hand. I'm so used to the feeling of a cool, lifeless touch, I'm not sure how he will feel under my grasp.

I slide my hand against his, and shivers shoot through me. They sting up my arm and through my chest until they penetrate my heart. I gasp, focusing on his soft, supple skin. Everywhere his skin touches mine tingles. My skin hums, his vibrating caress erupting life within me and through me.

His hand is so warm. The moment I wrap my fingers around it, I gasp. I can feel the blood rushing through his veins. His skin is so thin, I swear I can actually *see* the life inside him. It's warm and blue, and I know it tastes so good. I run my tongue against the points of my fangs and imagine his blood turning from blue to bright red right before my eyes.

"You're not around humans much, huh?" Holland asks with a chuckle.

It's enough to break my concentration. I jerk my hand away and stumble backward. Malik is still behind me, and I fall against him. He groans inwardly, but I hear his frustration. He's probably annoyed that I couldn't focus during our training session because of my excitement for this very moment, yet I'm acting like a total wreck now that it's finally here.

It never occurred to me that this would be my first encounter with mortal flesh. I didn't realize the hold blood still has over me. Succumbing to a liquid diet was hard for me. It took weeks just to get comfortable making my own breakfast. I feel like I'm recessing back into the Ava I used to be—the timid, unsure creature I was the first night Jasik brought me here. I don't want to be her anymore. I want confidence and strength.

Realizing I have yet to answer him, I nod. "Yes, I'm Ava."

Holland smiles again. "It's nice to meet you, Ava. I hear you're having a problem."

"I, uh, yeah. It's kind of a unique situation . . . I guess," I say.

Holland nods. "Well, you weren't human."

I shake my head. "No."

"I've been thinking about you a lot, actually, ever since ..." Holland clears his throat. "Um, ever since Jeremiah called."

I don't miss his hesitation when he mentions his ex-boyfriend. Unsurprisingly so, Hikari was right. There are definitely unresolved feelings there. Selfishly, my first thought isn't that I hope these two lovebirds reconcile. All I can think about is myself and how I hope this won't be a distraction while Holland and I work through this.

"Why don't I take your bags and get you set up in the guest room. You and Ava can take a seat in the solarium to chat," Malik says. He walks around me to grab Holland's only bag. Without waiting for a response, he picks up the suitcase and turns back toward the staircase. As he walks past me, we make eye contact. Everything he needs to say is said in that one glance.

Figure this out, and don't mess up.

I turn back to the others. Most of the vampires have cleared out, making promises to catch up later. Soon, I'm standing alone with Holland and Jasik. With Malik no longer standing behind me, anchoring me to this spot in time, that rush of uneasiness comes back.

In true sire fashion, Jasik is quick to come to my side. It's as if he sensed my uncertainty. I smile up at him, offering him silent thanks. He nods at me, understanding. Instinctively, I grab on to his hand, lacing our fingers together. A tingle shoots through me. It's not a dissimilar feeling than what I just experienced with Holland, but my reaction to it has definitely changed. With Holland, I am fearful, unsure, and on guard. Jasik's touch gives me a rush of life. He makes me feel stronger, wiser, and beautiful. He looks at me with such appreciation and thoughtfulness.

Holland clears his throat, and I jerk my gaze back to him. Something about being so close to Jasik makes my head foggy, but I need to focus. Holland was asked to come for a reason, and I need to remember that. Without him, I'm surely doomed.

"I'm glad to see everything is the same," Holland says, a coy smile crossing his face as he looks from our hands to our eyes. He winks at Jasik as he turns on his heels and enters the parlor. I gnaw on my lower lip at his insinuation and pull my hand free from Jasik's. I don't dare look at him as I follow Holland.

The parlor smells musty. It smells like the many books encased in the shelves all around this room. Nothing in the world smells like a book. If it were possible for knowledge to have a smell, it would smell just like this—stale, stuffy, and a little dank. Paper has that airless scent to it.

A large stone fireplace is centered against the only wall not covered with bookcases or the large bay window to my right. A few vampires are camped out in the room. Some are reading, some are talking, but none are playing the game of chess on the table in front of the bay window. During my second night here, Jasik informed me that he and Malik have been playing that game for *years*. Malik refuses to make a move because it's a losing game for him. So it sits, gathering dust, much like my old room at Mamá's house.

The parlor opens to the sitting room on my left, but it also has an entrance to the solarium, which extends along the right side of the house. We can enter the solarium from the parlor, sitting room, and dining room, and there are even two entrances from outside—one at the front of the house and one at the back. It's a massive L-shaped room with stained-glass windows, plants that thrive at night, and many seating areas.

Thankfully, for the time being, no one is here but us. The last thing I want is an obvious eavesdropper.

After we enter the solarium, I pull out a chair at my favorite seating area and take a seat. From where I'm seated, I can see straight through to the backyard garden. The first time I ventured back there, I was jumping out of Jasik's bedroom window in a sad attempt to prove my worthiness. I didn't have a chance to appreciate the plant beds or the way the trees cluster together. I barely noticed how close we were to the sea, but now I can hear the waves crashing, smell the salty air, feel the tingle of mist against my cheeks. It's hard to imagine living somewhere other than Darkhaven.

I eye Jasik curiously. It's been a long time since the first night he brought me into this room. We were sitting at a table at the other end of the solarium, and after giving me a quick tour of the manor, he offered me words of wisdom and shared secrets from his past. I can't help but think about how he and Malik died all those years ago. Talking about it doesn't seem to bother him anymore, but I think he still misses his family. I wonder if Mamá will still have her hold on me even after she's gone.

"You mentioned you've been thinking about Ava's situation," Jasik says as he takes a seat beside me. He doesn't seem to notice that I've been gawking at him ever since I sat down. The legs of his chair scrape against the tile floor, and I cringe at the sound. A shiver rushes through me, and I gnaw on my lower lip, eagerly awaiting Holland's response.

He nods. "I have. Vampires were once human. It's possible there are other witch-turned-vampires in existence, but honestly, I've never met one. But this is where your situation is rather unique."

"I've never met someone like Ava either," Jasik agrees.

A rush of warmth washes over me. Jasik doesn't just say he hasn't met another witch-turned-vampire; he says he's never met someone *like me*. I understand the hidden meaning in his words, and something sparks inside me. I reach for him and place my hand on his knee. He looks down at me, smiling.

Holland notices my gesture, even though my hand and Jasik's knee are hidden beneath the table, but continues talking. "It's safe to say this isn't common. After all, witches and vampires tend to steer clear of each other."

I nod and think about the lessons I learned while growing up. I was taught to believe vampires were evil, soulless creatures who needed to be killed. I suppose that's true for rogue vampires, but not for the others. I imagine Holland experienced these same lessons. I wonder how many other times he and I were led astray by our covens. Is this why Holland left his coven? Did he discover their betrayal?

"If you think of vampirism like a virus, then this virus attacks human cells, morphing them into something else. This is the transition process a human experiences during the blood swap. The vampire's blood sort of . . . takes over and replaces the human cells with enhanced vampire cells. The human then becomes a vampire."

I nod and shrug. "Sure, I guess that makes sense."

"Well, as a witch, your cells were already changed by something," Holland continues.

I furrow my brow. "By what?"

"Magic."

"So what does that mean?" Jasik asks. He leans forward, resting his elbows against the tabletop. I mimic his position because I'm equally interested. I've never thought of witchcraft in this way, but it makes sense. Witches *are* human. They're mortal creatures, but something separates them from being *just* human—*magic*. I think Holland is on to something.

"Honestly, I'm not sure, and I could be wrong, but I think this is why Ava is . . . different," Holland says. He brushes hair from his eyes and offers a sad smile. It's as if he's apologizing for not having better news.

"So I'm not a vampire?" I ask.

"Oh, no, you're *definitely* a vampire. You have the pale skin, the red eyes, and I'm guessing you drink blood and have enhanced senses. You have all the traits of being a vampire—"

"But . . . the other night—" I begin, interrupting Holland.

"But I don't think you're *just* a vampire. I think you're something *more*," Holland continues.

I want to shout from the rooftops that I agree with him. *Of course* I'm something more. We established that the moment I tapped into magic. But *what* am I? And what does this mean? Will I ever be normal? Do I have all vampire traits or just some? Will I be able to access magic again, or was that a one-time thing? Questions clutter my head, and I feel like I may lose my mind if I don't get some answers.

"Basically, you think she's . . . mixed? Part vampire and part witch?" Jasik clarifies.

Holland is quiet for a moment as he considers Jasik's question. "I think she might be. I can't be sure, though. I've never met anyone like you, and I don't really have a coven to reach out to for guidance."

I want to ask about his former coven, but I don't. Still, the desire to do so burns within me. I'm not sure why I'm so nosy with him, but I ache to know more about his past, about what drove him away from his coven and how he's surviving on his own. He's so similar to me, yet so different.

"I don't either," I say.

My voice is raw, soft, and I sound utterly pathetic. The pain from losing my coven comes in waves. Loss is funny that way. There are days I'm so strong that I never question my ability to carry on without them. I consider it their loss, not mine. But then the sun rises and sets on another day, and once again, their betrayal burns in the pit of my gut. I ache to see them, to be with them again.

It's been six weeks since my coven deemed me forsaken, and in that time, the only thing that's changed is my attitude toward the vampires. On the days I want to return home, it would only be to visit, because I can't bring myself to leave Jasik or Malik or Hikari or Jeremiah.

As much as it pains me to know my own mother has abandoned me, that isn't the worst of it. That honor goes to the days when I wake up having forgotten what happened six weeks ago. I open my eyes to see a new room, and I remember all over again that I'm not in the house I grew up in. I'm not friends with Liv anymore. I'm not Mamá's daughter or a witch who is part of a coven.

This loss is similar to the death of someone I love. Even on the days I *know* what happened and am strong enough to forgive them, I still feel like it never should have happened. I feel like, even though I'm a vampire, I should be able to call Mamá and ask for help when I need her.

But I can't.

Mamá will never forgive me.

When Jasik clasps his hand around mine, I realize I've been staring into space, absentmindedly lost in my own thoughts. I blink away the memories that plague my existence and smile to reassure him that I'm okay.

"Ava, I might not know what's going on, but I'm more than happy to stay here and help you. I won't leave until you can control it," Holland says.

✦

Jeremiah crashes into the room, sending us spiraling back to reality. He's dressed in his patrol gear—dark jeans and jacket, with a dagger strapped to his waist. His hands are caked with dried blood, and his jeans are ripped, exposing dirty skin beneath. Clearly he was fighting, and it didn't go well.

"What is it?" Jasik asks, standing abruptly, scraping his chair against the tile. I wince at the sound.

"We have a serious problem," Jeremiah says.

Holland clears his throat and sits straighter. He's staring at Jeremiah, desperately trying to get his attention but not succeeding. With each passing second, Holland begins to sink farther down into his chair. My heart hurts for him. I know how hard it is to so desperately desire someone's affection and not receive it.

"What happened?" Jasik asks.

"I was patrolling, and I ran into rogues," Jeremiah says. "I chased them down, fighting the last one almost into town. They're getting more brazen."

Jasik nods and exhales sharply. "I was afraid of this. Darkhaven is a small village. They don't have access to as much food unless they leave the forest."

"That's not our only problem," Jeremiah says. He eyes me cautiously without continuing.

I cross my arms over my chest, preparing to hold myself.

Something inside me doesn't want to hear what Jeremiah has to say. I know it won't be good news, and I have an inkling it's going to make things very bad for me. Even so, I say, "What is it?"

Jeremiah glances back at Jasik. Something crosses between the two. The silence stretches for only a few seconds, but it feels like hours. My annoyance grows, and I bite my tongue until I can't any longer.

"What happened? Just tell me!" I shout. At this point, I'm growing more frantic and readying myself for the worst.

"I overheard something unsettling," Jeremiah says carefully.

"Just tell us," Jasik says. Even he sounds frustrated that Jeremiah feels he needs to be so cautious around me.

"A witch from Darkhaven was taken."

FIVE

By the time Jeremiah returned home and informed us of a missing Darkhaven witch, the sun was soon to rise. Waiting until the following eve was soul-crushing. I couldn't sleep, so I didn't even try. All I could do was envision my former coven missing another witch. This has to be a devastating blow.

After abandoning me during what was probably my weakest, most desperate moment, the witches didn't deserve my help, but my pride wouldn't prevent me from offering the aid they so desperately need right now.

My bedroom is dark, dank. I once found this space inviting, welcoming, and vibrant. It was full of life and love—a place I could see myself living as the many years came and went. I had an eternity, but I didn't need that much time to call this place home. Amicia's Victorian-style manor had grown on me, but now, my comfort mocks me.

My beige bedspread is murky and dark. The sheer white fabric that twists around the bed posts and encases the mattress feels more like a prison than a paradise.

The room's dark-blue walls are closing in on me, and I wipe my moist palms against my thighs to dry them. I'm nervous about facing the witches again, and I fear what they may do when I show up with a herd of vampires. The fact that we had to wait another day isn't helping my tension. I fear for the missing witch's safety.

I pace my room, replaying last night's conversation on a loop in my mind. Jeremiah was worried I would lash out, mindless and steadfast in my decision to protect what was once familiar to me. I can't fault his logic. That was my first thought. My innate reaction to protect the witches is nestled so deep within me, I fear I may never shake it.

I know this is why Amicia is worried about a former witch living with her vampires. My hatred for them was instilled at birth. What she doesn't understand is that this manor feels more like home than the house I lived in with Mamá. The last thing I want to do is hurt the vampires.

After walking in circles and staring at the hardwood floors, I stop in front of a corner mirror and stare at my reflection. Far too many hours have passed since the witch went missing, and all I can do is imagine her face even as I look at my own.

My reflection betrays my greatest fear. I blink, and I no longer see myself; I see Mamá or Liv. I pray they're not among the missing. I pray someone else was taken. I hate myself for even thinking it, for wishing it, but not enough to take it back. I can be selfish for once in my life . . . right?

I blink and look at my reflection again, and I see a stranger. No longer haunted by my family and friends, I wonder who she is. Is this the witch's face? Is she still alive? Is this her or just some cruel trick my mind is playing on me?

As a spirit witch, I had access to magic even our elders didn't understand. At night I would dream, and the next day, what I assumed were dreams were visions of future events. Sometimes I would enter the dreams of other spirit users, like Mamá. Now that I know I'm not *just* a vampire, maybe I'm actually seeing the missing witch. Maybe my powers are growing, and . . .

I shake my head and exhale sharply.

"You're losing your mind, Ava," I say aloud.

I can't let my fear, confusion, and anxiety affect me like this. The second the sun sets and the world is cast in darkness, the vampires and I are going to the witches. I need to be on my A-game if I expect to convince them to let us help find who's missing.

I don't know her face or her name or how she ended up in a critical situation, but I know she's scared. She doesn't think she'll be saved. I know this, even without speaking to her or looking into her eyes, because this is how I felt that night. The vampires saved us from the rogues, and even as I begged for help, deep down, I didn't believe Jasik would save me. After all, we were supposed to be mortal enemies, and even if we could set aside our mutual distrust, I was sure I was too far gone.

I think about the witches. I know Mamá is pacing the room, just like I am, but her face is void of emotion, as it always was. She is an expert at concealing her emotions. She once told me this made her a better parent. She said I needed her to be strong after Papá died. She said I needed a father more than a mother. I'm certain this is why our relationship has always been strained. When I wanted to break, she wouldn't let me, even if all I really needed was a good cry.

If nothing else, Mamá made me an excellent warrior. Removing my own emotions to fight vampires has always come easy to me. I never feared death or facing a stronger opponent. Unfortunately, the pendulum swings both ways. I also never experienced life until the moment I died. The moment I drank Jasik's blood and tapped into a part of myself I never knew was hidden.

"*Mamá, puedes escucharme?*" I ask if she can hear me, but I know she cannot.

I close my eyes and listen to my gut. Deep down to the depths of my soul, I know the witches need me right now, even if they won't be able to admit it. I can feel their pain and confusion. I sense it like I sense the fall of the sun, the rise of the moon, the change of the seasons.

I envision the witches and predict their plan. Having been a witch myself, I know exactly what they plan to do, and the realization that war is inevitable shakes me to my core. I squeeze my eyes shut until a shooting pain explodes behind my lids. I shake away the images that force their way into my mind. I don't want to see a dead witch or the bloodbath in the wake of their search for the missing.

Opening my eyes, I finally see myself in the mirror. My crimson irises are bright, but my eyes are sunken and dark from lack of sleep. My skin is pale, my small frame eerily gaunt and frail. I look as though I haven't slept or eaten in days. I know this isn't true, but my emotional internal battle is wreaking havoc on my mind, body, and soul.

"*Mamá, por favor, déjame ayudarte.*" I know she can't hear me, but I beg her to let me help nonetheless. Darkhaven shouldn't lose another witch to the vampires. As much as I'm starting to enjoy the perks of being a vampire, I wouldn't wish this curse on anyone. No one should live to watch their ancestors age and die, all the while knowing an eternity alone is inevitable.

After several seconds of receiving no answer, I decide my powers are not advancing. I step back with a huff, providing enough space between the mirror and me to properly assess myself.

"It's time I focus on what I *can* change," I say aloud.

I can't forget anything. This is too important. I complete

a mental checklist of the necessary items before I leave my room to join the others downstairs. I can hear the whispers of a waking house, and I'm certain everyone in the manor heard me talking to myself. Thankfully, I'm not worried about appearing mentally unstable, even though the thought of a missing witch is killing me on the inside.

Much like my current mood, my hair is so dark it's almost black. It's pulled back into a tight ponytail, and any loose strands are tucked behind my ears and pinned in place. Tonight, I can't afford even the slightest distraction, like loose hair poking me in the eyes as I fight whatever beast is holding the witch hostage.

I slip on my combat boots and double knot the laces. As usual, my pants are tucked inside. The stretchy material makes hunting and fighting rogues easy work. Like the others, I tend to wear the same style clothes for hunting—cropped military-style jacket, combat boots, black T-shirt, and dark pants. I want to blend into the shadows but also hide my extremely noticeable pale skin from any human onlookers.

I pat the side of my jacket, searching for the familiar groove of my hidden stake. It brings me comfort knowing it's the one thing from my past that still watches over me.

Unconsciously, I walk to my bedside table and open the drawer to display a thin black box. I remove it and glance at its contents. Running a finger along the edge of the jewelry box, I stare at the silver cross Papá gave me before he died. So long ago, I watched with vision blurred by tears as Mamá carried me out of the woods while Papá stayed behind to fight the vampires. I remember his blast of fire magic as he set the world aflame.

He never came home.

I wipe the single tear that falls, close the lid, and place the jewelry box back in the drawer. Without another thought, I leave my bedroom.

I'm drinking my third mug of blood before Jasik finds me in the kitchen. He strolls in and offers me a weak smile. His skin is paler than usual, and his brown hair is messily tousled atop his head. He runs a hand through it, and I've come to understand it's a nervous tic of his. I wonder what is making him wary—me or visiting the witches.

Dark circles under his eyes make his crimson irises pop. I'm guessing he didn't sleep last night either. If the others are just as exhausted, convincing the witches we're assets is going to be a greater challenge than I initially expected. These are the moments I miss things like coffee. I'm guessing we all need a caffeine boost.

To avoid speaking, I slurp loudly, and Jasik grabs a bag of blood from the refrigerator to fill a glass. He pops his mug into the microwave and turns to face me. Leaning against the counter, he crosses his arms over his chest and waits for me to speak. I know he wants me to break our silence first, but I don't want to debate this anymore. I'm tired of talking and waiting and not doing anything. I want action. I want to punch something. Of all the days for Malik to cancel training...

To avoid eye contact, I stare at the rows of empty cabinetry surrounding Jasik. They're utterly useless. As vampires, we need two things: a stocked fridge and a cabinet of microwave-safe mugs. That means our rather large kitchen is barren.

I glance back at Jasik, and his gaze burns into my own.

Last night, the vampires took a vote on whether or not we will aid the witches. Jasik sided with me, but I know he only did that because of our bond. The vampires don't want to help the witches, but they do want to eliminate the rogue who took her. It took far too long for me to convince them killing the rogue and helping the missing witch are the same task.

To eliminate the rogue, we must help the witches, and in the end, the vampires agreed I would go to the witches at sundown, even if they weren't coming with me. They ultimately agreed to help only because I'm too stubborn to walk away.

Now, there's a gnawing sensation in my gut. I don't like arguing with the vampires, and I feel like I've betrayed them by being so adamant about helping my former coven. Jasik never said anything, but I could see confusion and pain in his eyes. When I first arrived, I made it clear that I was only here for self-preservation. I had every intention of returning to my coven once I learned to control my blood lust. It's easier now, and I no longer feel that desire to return home. But does he know that?

The longer I think about our situation, the more my head hurts. I close my eyes and rub my temples. Since I have no access to herbs to create a healing elixir, I mentally prepare one by using a mortar and pestle to grind eucalyptus, lavender, and lemon balm. I'd fill a tea bag with the contents and inhale the steam as it steeped. Already, I feel my headache easing.

"Are you all right?"

I open my eyes to find Jasik beside me. His brow is furrowed, his cloudy irises laced with concern.

I nod. "Just tired. I didn't sleep."

He smiles at me, and the world slips away. My exhaustion, pain, and anxiety melt, and I feel rejuvenated again. I'm confident in myself and our plan to aid the witches, to find the rogues who've taken her and make sure no one will ever be harmed again. I don't worry about Jasik or the others, and I know, in time, they'll understand they made the right decision to help the witches.

I don't miss my rather abrupt mood change. I hate that Jasik has so much power over my emotions, but I love that even the darkest days brighten when he's around. He makes my heart ache and my mind flutter in all the best ways.

"You're stronger than you know, Ava. Even a few sleepless nights can't hinder your strength."

His comforting words wrap around me and bounce inside my head. I hear him over and over again, believing him each time. I know I'm strong, and I know I can handle this, but knowing he believes in me gives me that extra boost I need after last night's insomnia.

"Everything will be okay," Jasik says.

I smile. "Promise?"

Even though he answers me, he doesn't need to respond. I already know the truth of his words.

Together, we will save the witch.

✦

It didn't take long to reach Mamá's house, and now that I'm here, mere feet away from the very last place I saw my coven, I want to leave. I'm scared to knock on the door as if nothing happened, and I'm still angry with them for forsaking me. What's most confusing is even after all of that, I still have it in my heart to love and miss them. If I don't get my emotions in check, I'll never make it to my next birthday.

Jasik is standing beside me. He laces his fingers through mine and holds my hand. Offering a comforting squeeze, I glance up at him and smile. I nod to let him know I'm okay and totally not having a mental breakdown after seeing my old house again.

Of course, this isn't the first time I've been back. He doesn't know I was here a couple of weeks ago. I watched my former coven complete their full moon ritual exactly one month after they sent me to my death. I never told the other vampires because I didn't expect them to understand. I may hate the witches for what they did to me, but they're still my only living blood relatives. I *had* to watch over them, especially during that ritual.

I glance over my shoulder to find Malik, Jeremiah, and Hikari watching us. By now, they're used to our public displays of affection, and they understand our bond. Jasik sired me, and I'm forever indebted to him because of it. But what they don't know is there's something more here.

A spark of attraction flows between us, tethering his soul to mine. If the world would stop spinning for just a second, I would spend some time trying to understand what's developing between us, but whenever I have even a moment's peace, either another crisis crashes through our door or Malik insists on a training session. I wish he had more faith in my previous training, but he doesn't believe the witches taught me enough to save my neck against rogue vampires. I suppose he may be right. The last rogue I fought nearly killed me with my own stake.

I turn back toward my old house. We're standing in the backyard, just beyond the fence that separates Mamá's property and the surrounding woods of Darkhaven. We haven't yet dared to venture onto her property.

I can hear the bustle of movement coming from inside the house. A knot forms in my throat, and I swallow it down. My hands are clammy, and my heart is racing. It's so loud in my chest, I'm surprised I can hear the outside world. Jasik squeezes my hand reassuringly, but I ignore him.

I stare at the house. I grew up here, but it seems so unfamiliar now. Papá built this house from cedar planks. Over time, the sand-colored wood turned a dark-gray color and has remained that way ever since. Mamá never painted it after Papá died. In fact, Mamá refused to make any changes to the house, forcing us to live in a stagnant place that's been frozen in time.

Sometimes, I think Mamá thought Papá would return, as if that night in the woods never happened and he's just been away. Every year at this time, Abuela visits distant relatives, leaving the care of our coven in Mamá's hands. Maybe she believes Papá is with her and will return with our high priestess.

Or maybe Mamá does believe it happened and she wants him to come home, even if he … turned. I like to think she would take him back even if he were like me now. But I know she wouldn't.

"They won't be happy we're here," I say softly.

No one speaks, but I hear the hiccup in their breath as it catches. They're waiting for me to continue, to explain exactly what we've gotten ourselves into.

"There were thirteen members in my coven. Without me, twelve remain, but anyone could be here tonight. We weren't the only coven in Darkhaven," I say. I pull my hand free from Jasik's and rub my moist palms together. The anticipation of seeing Mamá again is making me nervous.

"Everything will be okay," Jasik says. His voice is soft to not to alert the witches inside. The windows are open, with cool breezes rushing indoors each time the wind picks up. I wish it were the other way. I'd kill to smell the scents of home. Sage is likely burning... or maybe Mamá's favorite incense. She might be cooking stew or running a lavender bath. It's strange the things you miss when you're gone.

"What if they attack?" Hikari asks. She's still a good two or three strides behind me. Her voice is soft, squeaky. I hear her grunt, and I turn in time to see Jeremiah pulling his arm back. He just elbowed her in the side.

I face the house again and scan the dark windows upstairs. The bedrooms and altar room are on the second floor, but from the commotion inside, everyone is downstairs, likely planning their attack to recover the missing witch.

"I won't be able to protect you from the fire witches," I say. Silently, I think, *because I'll be too busy protecting myself.* The witches won't stop at my allies. They will come for my heart too. I gnaw on my lower lip. Am I ready for this?

"If we want to help, we need to move quickly," Malik says. "We only have until dawn."

I nod, exhale sharply, and take the first step toward my old life. Unfortunately, the road to an unkind death is filled with good intentions.

The moment I cross the threshold into the backyard, a brain-piercing shriek permeates from the house. I scream as I cover my ears with my palms. Falling to my knees, tears streak down my cheeks as lightning-fast pain spreads like wildfire from my brain to my heart to my limbs. I can't see or hear or think. I'm surrounded by darkness, an eternal pit of nothing but sheer agony. I imagine this is what hell must be like—

constant, everlasting, brutal *torture*.

When it finally stops, I slowly open my eyes and find myself in the fetal position on the ground. The other vampires are beside me, cowering, crawling to their knees. Blood streaks from their ears in steady streams and pools on the ground. Whatever attacked me affected them too.

I wipe away my tears to find my hands bloody. I stare, shocked, and frantically scan my surroundings for Jasik. His face is stained with blood as well. As the others begin to face me, I see more blood stripes slashed across faces. What I assumed were tears was actually blood seeping from my eyes.

"You're not welcome here," someone says.

I blink away the blood that still clouds my vision and search the yard for our attacker. Mamá stands several feet away from me, her coven behind her. Even from afar, she towers over me.

"Mamá?" I breathe.

"*No tartamudeé, niña,*" she said.

"*Que pasó?*" I ask. "What happened?" I repeat myself and feel a pang of sadness. Mamá used to repeat herself in both languages all the time when we had visitors. I wonder if she still does.

"I said, you are not welcome here. Leave. Now." Her words are firm, her tone sharp, and I am certain she will unleash whatever hell magic she just used on us if we don't comply.

"We came to help," I whisper.

"Help us? How?" another witch says. I don't recognize her. She's tall, thin, with wild red locks that fall well below her shoulders. Her curls are tight and natural, and her blue eyes are tinged with slate gray. They're cold, lifeless, and her attitude is fueled by her hatred for all that I am.

"The missing witch," I say softly as I try to stand, but I'm pushed back down again by an air witch. The rush of wind slams into my body, and I flop onto the ground in a heap. The other vampires still haven't moved. They're waiting for me to control this situation, to convince the witches that we're worthy of helping them.

"We didn't come to fight," I seethe. I grind my teeth, a sudden burst of annoyance rushing through me.

"And we don't need your help," someone else says. I don't bother searching for the speaker. Instead, I stare straight at Mamá. Her long dark hair rustles in the breeze. Her eyes are dark and swollen, as if she's been crying. I don't trick myself into believing she sheds tears for me. It's for the missing witch.

I gasp, a horrifying thought creeping its way into my mind. "Mamá, who was taken? *Quien falta?*" I ask. I don't know any other witch she would cry for besides Liv, my former best friend. I never got to say goodbye to her or explain my side of the story. I assume she hates me and decided it was best to let go of our friendship.

I never tried to contact her after I changed, but that was when I thought witches and vampires couldn't live together. Holland and Jeremiah made it work. They knew each other intimately, so why couldn't I befriend Liv again? If she'll let me explain, I can prove to her that I'm no danger to her or any other human.

"*A usted no le incumbe. Déjanos!*" Mamá yells. Her hands are balled at her sides, her knuckles turning a vicious shade of white by the sheer force of her fury.

But I will not leave. I refuse to back down.

"Stop this! This *is* my business too!" I shout. I stand so swiftly the other witches jump backward, flush against the side of the house. One girl stumbles so far, she trips over the sliding door frame and falls onto the kitchen tile. She shimmies back, her brown hair a chaotic mess across her face. When she pushes back her erratic mane and makes eye contact, a rush of relief washes over me.

Liv.

My best friend.

She's not missing.

But then, who was taken? Who would make Mamá cry? Or has she mourned losing her only child?

Before I can think this through, I notice the horrified look creasing Liv's usually pristine face. She's shocked to see me and disgusted by what I've become. Her only encounter with vampires was with me, and every time we fought them, I coached her. I made her fear for her life. I forced her to believe vampires are evil. And now I am one.

"Liv . . ." My voice is a whisper.

I take one step toward the witches but am stopped when a pain greater than anything I've ever experienced envelops my entire body. The world erupts into commotion, and my senses take control.

Lights flash, burning my eyes.

My allies scream, but their pain is quickly muffled by my overworked senses.

I bellow in pain, my muscles tightening into solid knots.

My senses rapid-fire through my system, offering no sign of relief.

Everything hurts, so I stumble forward, gasping for breath. Blood seeps from my mouth and splatters down my chin. I fall to my knees and glance down at my hands. No longer is my skin pale white. It is stained with blood—*my blood*. It pools in my hands and slips through my fingers, forming a puddle on the grass. The juxtaposition of my crimson blood and the earthy green ground is jarring.

My heart is beating steadily in my head, but it's softening with each desperate attempt to feed my body its only life source. My head lulls forward until I'm staring straight at the ground.

Slumped over, I understand why the vampires are screaming, why my chest aches, why I'm coated in blood, and why it's getting more and more difficult to keep my eyes open.

Protruding from my gut is the jagged edge of a long tree branch. The bark is slick with my flesh, and my wound is steadily dripping. My clothes are drenched and make a squishing sound as I fall onto my side. I grab on to the branch and wrap my fingers around it.

Sharp pain radiates from my lungs. I'm certain death is imminent because I feel the wood splintering off, scratching against the throbbing muscles in my chest. I so desperately want to lie on my back, but I can't. Something stops me.

I reach behind me and run my fingers against the opposite end of the branch. The wood piercing my chest must be several feet in length and is protruding from my back. I squeeze until it snaps.

I double-hand the branch at my chest and try to pull it free. The wood budges only slightly, but I scream in agony. The sound escaping my lips can't possibly be my voice.

It scratches against bone, a pulse-pounding scrape that radiates through my entire body. I can't shake the feeling, and I replay the sound over and over again in my mind.

Feeling weak and light-headed, I collapse and roll onto my back. I arch forward when my wound comes into contact with solid earth, and I inhale sharply, my lungs stinging against the foreign substance that's making its way deeper into my torso.

I need to remove the branch or I won't heal, but even the slightest budge is mind-numbing.

The moon and stars are bright above me, but something blocks them. I blink until my eyes focus, hoping Jasik or even Mamá has come to my aid. Instead, I stare into his familiar crimson irises.

He smiles, a deviant glare in his eyes that sends shivers down my spine.

He is the vampire who haunts my dreams, the one who stole my life from me. I knew he would come for me, that his lackeys' constant defeat would prove too much for his pride.

"You missed my heart," I hiss under my breath. I clench my jaw shut, struggling to hide my pain.

"Or maybe I have you right where I want you," he says. His eyes betray his anger, but he chuckles.

Before I can respond, the rogue vampire grabs on to the branch that's bulging from my chest and yanks it free.

SIX

The gaping hole in my chest steals my breath. I choke out vague threats as my body struggles to heal itself. Flesh tethers together, threading new life from old, and the rogue vampire stands over me, mocking my pain.

He says something inaudible, and even though my senses are overloaded, I feel stronger. With each passing second, I slip further away from death and back to my painful reality.

I'm not paying attention to the rogue, and that must anger him. He kicks my side—once, twice, three times. I hear ribs snap as the sharp point of his boot makes contact with already wounded flesh. I scream through closed lips, hoping he can't sense how much pain I'm in. I can show no sign of weakness.

"Ava, get up!"

Someone shouts at me, but my vision is blurred. I try to blink away the pain, but it's no use. Just when I think I'm free, my assailant hits me again and again.

I roll onto my stomach and try to crawl away. Digging my fingers into the cold earth, I burrow beneath the grass, grabbing on to the land, and pull myself closer to Mamá's house. I need to escape my attacker and allow myself to properly heal.

I hear him laughing behind me, and I feel his approach. It feels like a thousand needles pricking my skin at once, and there's nothing I can do to stop it from happening.

You need to get up!

I scream at myself internally, and I struggle to stand. By the time I manage to lift myself on all fours, the rogue is beside me, thrusting his leg into my side. He makes impact, and I'm flung several feet away. I hear the distinct crunch of my ribs cracking. A broken shard stings at my side, slicing through thin layers of muscle.

"I'm impressed that you so easily thwarted my earlier attacks, little one," the rogue says. He licks his lips when I look at him, as if he's already envisioning tasting me. The thought nauseates me.

The moonlight beams off his greasy bald head. He wipes the sweat that beads along his forehead and walks closer to me. He's wearing a tight black T-shirt that looks about three sizes too small. His muscles strain against the fabric as he reaches down and grabs my neck. His hands are large enough to almost completely clasp his fingers around me.

Before I can react, I'm airborne. He's lifting me closer to him and slams my frail body against the side of the house. With both hands, he grabs on to my throat and squeezes until I cannot breathe. I gasp for air, scratching at his hands, drawing blood from his skin and a smile from his lips.

He leans in close and whispers in my ear. His breath is hot against my flesh, and it makes me squirm beneath his grasp. "I've been waiting for this moment since the first time I saw you. Do you remember that day in the cemetery? I watched from the shadows as you fought those vampires with admirable conviction, but your confidence has gotten the best of you now. I've been watching, waiting, enjoying how you slowly went mad from fear."

He leans back and slams my body against the wood siding

again and again. The house protests, a dull ache cascading through its walls and out the open windows. If he wanted to, he could force me through, and what would happen then? Would he stop at killing me, or would he finish off my coven as retribution for all the men I killed while he played his twisted mind game?

I thrust my hands up, jabbing his wrists, but he doesn't release me. Instead, he laughs at my pathetic attempt to free myself. To no avail, I try again and again. Distraught and in desperate need of oxygen, I smash my forehead against his chin. He's too tall for a nose shot, and all I really accomplish is giving myself a splitting headache.

My chest burns, so I reach forward and shove my thumbs into his eye sockets. I dig deeply and nearly lose my breakfast as my nails squish into something soft. The rogue screams, and I fall to the ground. He covers his eyes with his hands, rubbing his fresh wounds, and I scurry across the ground, clutching my chest. Fresh oxygen is like acid in my lungs.

By the time I make it to my feet, someone is behind me. The rogue grabs on to me, wrapping his arms around my torso, caging me between his thick arms. I try to wiggle free, but it's no use. He's clasped his hands together, threading his fingers, and my arms are still dangling at my sides.

I feel his breath on my neck, and a jolt of electricity shoots through me. His fangs grace my skin, and I scream. He hasn't bitten down, but I've never felt so terrified in my life. I can't help but bellow for help. I jerk around, thrashing my head from side to side, back to front. I know the moment he sinks his fangs into my neck, I'm dead. A vampire can drain his victim in seconds, though most prefer to treasure the moment and drink slowly. I know he plans to suck me dry in the blink of an eye and then turn to my friends.

"Can I tell you a secret, Ava?" the vampire taunts.

I'm still screaming and thrashing and praying to whatever god or goddess will hear me. I ball my fists and try to punch his legs, but I can't move my wrists more than an inch or two. I try to scratch at his legs, but his jeans are too thick to penetrate. I slam my head back once, twice, and then again. Finally, I make contact. I feel a hot, sticky substance squirt onto the back of my neck and trickle down my spine. I shiver as it seeps beneath my T-shirt. The rogue laughs and then leans forward and wipes his nose along the curve of my neck. His blood coats me, and bile rises in my throat. I feel *marked*.

The rogue latches his tongue onto my ear and sucks it into his mouth. I shriek as he bites down, drawing blood. He pulls away before I can shout for him to stop, to release me, that he will die for this. I've never felt so abused, so violated.

"There is no witch," the vampire whispers.

I'm silent. I stop fighting and fall limp in his arms. I lean against him, and he waits for his words to sink in. Immediately, I understand what he's admitting.

There is no missing witch.

This was a setup.

This was part of his sick game.

No longer fearing for my own safety, I take in the scene before me. He's holding me so I face the massacre. Rogues are everywhere. The bloodbath ensuing mirrors the one shed during that fatal full moon ritual two months ago.

Witches are dead, their lifeless carcasses staring at me accusingly. They ask me why I let this happen, why I didn't protect them, why I came here to begin with.

I search the bodies for Mamá, for Liv, but I only see

strangers. The woman from earlier is among them. Her blue eyes are now completely void of life and have turned slate gray. Her curly red hair is frayed and coppery, lifeless. Her skin is pale white save for her crimson neck, where two tiny pinpricks betray the vampire's mark.

Tears burn behind my eyes as I search for my friends. I see Hikari and Jeremiah, but Malik and Jasik are missing. If they were killed, they would have turned to dust. There wouldn't be a body to mourn and bury. I wouldn't be able to find their lifeless corpse and know the truth—that they died trying to protect everything they stood for. They would simply be *gone*.

For the second time in my short life, his fangs pierce my skin and dig into my flesh. They penetrate muscle, ripping what's been newly threaded. I gasp, sucking in a sharp breath before I'm flung from his arms and soaring through the air. For several steady seconds, I'm flying, no longer rooted in what is surely my living hell. But like all flying creatures, I eventually land.

I fall against a solid surface and wince as my broken body makes contact with something hard. Pain surges through me, and I squeeze my eyes shut until it passes. When I open them, I see Jasik staring down at me. I'm cradled in his arms. Relief washes over him as I whisper his name, and I pull him down to me. I wrap my arms around his neck and bury my face into his skin. He smells like peppermint and sage and . . . *blood*.

I push away until he releases me. Turning, I search for the rogue. He's now battling with Malik, who must have helped Jasik tag-team him to free me. Malik is an expert warrior and easily matches the rogue's moves, but he is the weaker vampire. Rogues are naturally stronger predators, for they feed directly from humans. Fresh blood is coated in a living person's life force, and that essence resides in each drop. The moment this rogue gains the upper hand, Malik will surely succumb to the stronger predator.

"We have to help him!" I shout.

Before I can aid my friend, Jasik pulls me back. I yank my arm free, but he stops me again. I thrust my arm forward, striking Jasik in his chest, but I'm too weak to cause any real damage. He barely shifts under the weight of my attack.

"You must feed, Ava!" he shouts.

"There's no time!"

As I try to run away, I realize how weak I truly am. My limbs are heavy, my chest aches, my head is spinning... Jasik is right. I've lost too much blood, sustained too many injuries. I need to be at my best to help my friends. Until I feed, my body won't properly—or quickly—heal.

But how can I feed? There are no blood bags here, and I can't leave the battle to find a stray animal in the forest. Surely the witches won't offer sustenance. I glance back at Jasik, certain my eyes are betraying my fear and hunger.

As if reading my mind, Jasik pulls off his jacket and withdraws his dagger. He slides the blade across his wrist, and the sweetest aroma enters my nose. It's like nothing I've ever smelled before. My body twitches in response, and like a zombie, I walk toward him and latch on to his wrist.

Jasik doesn't need to tell me that this is taboo, that feeding from him won't sustain me for long, that doing this is going to change things between us. He doesn't tell me these things because they don't matter. I can't stop myself from tasting him. I accept his offering and sink my fangs into his flesh.

Feeding from a living—or even an undead—creature is nothing like sipping from a blood bag. I suppose that's why the vampires choose to drink from a mug. They've turned feeding into a stale, automatic experience. They've eliminated the predatory drive. But now, as I slice through Jasik's flesh, feeling his body firmly pressed against my own, feeding feels . . . different. It's exciting, arousing, and I never want it to end.

I latch on to Jasik's T-shirt and run my hand up and down the length of his chest. The harder I suck, the faster his heart beats. I listen to the steady thrusts of his overworked muscle and imagine sinking my fangs into it.

The chaos around us falls away, and silence envelops the world. I had no idea blood could have such control over me, over him, over our emotions. In the midst of a war, all I see is him.

Jasik whispers my name. His voice is soft, pleading, as if he's telling me I need to be the one to stop, that he isn't strong enough to pull away. The feeling of having such control over the one who granted me this life is euphoric.

I take one last hard suck, relishing in the way Jasik moans my name, and pull back. I stare into his eyes, and they're glowing. His crimson irises are shimmering and neon and full of such devotion and lust. He doesn't want me to stop. He wants me to feed from him until he takes his last breath. And I want to. I want to relish in his blood, in his body. I want to feel him give way to my strength.

He's so close. We breathe the same air. I lean against him, angling my head up, and he understands, leaning down. Our lips brush, and everything explodes.

Before we kiss, someone screams my name. I jerk away, stumbling backward until I fall on my butt. I look from the battle to Jasik and back again. My cheeks heat with embarrassment. I can't believe I was so caught up in my blood lust that I neglected to aid my friends. How could blood make me ignore the world around me so completely?

Malik screams a blood-curdling howl, and it has me pouncing to my feet in a flash. Jasik has already left me and joins his brother. He grabs on to Malik's arm and pulls him from the ground just as the rogue's fists come crashing down. The two miss each other by mere seconds.

A dagger is protruding from Malik's gut, and Jasik yanks it free. With these two safely away, I set my sights on the rogue vampire.

With the taste of Jasik's blood still on my lips, I charge the rogue, roaring like some wild beast with each step I take. My footfalls radiate through the earth and echo all around me.

In a flash, Jeremiah is in front of me. He takes a knee and throws his arms out before him. They're two solid slabs of muscle, and I know exactly what he expects me to do with them.

I run faster, putting every ounce of energy into my legs as I can. I leap, jump onto Jeremiah's arms, and he propels me forward. Once again, I'm flying. I spin through the air fast enough to surprise the rogue and plant a solid two feet against his chest. The force behind impact is so harsh, he is flung backward and doesn't stop until he slams into the base of a thick tree several dozen yards away.

Back on my feet, I unzip my jacket's inner pocket and unsheathe my stake. I withdraw it and clench it tightly in my hand. The rogue is jumping back to his feet in time to watch me point the sharp end directly at his heart. I smile, a wicked threat on the tip of my tongue, but he doesn't give me a chance to speak.

He's running toward me, and I pounce into the air,

curving my spine until I backflip right over him. When I land, I spin and thrust my leg outward once, twice. I swing my arms around and hit him over and over again. I use the stake as more than the deadly weapon it is. Each time I hit him with my right hand, the pointed dagger skids across his skin, leaving crimson slashes in its wake.

He lashes forward, desperately trying to grab on to me, but I'm too fast. I sidestep all of his attacks just like Malik taught me. If he weren't slowly bleeding to death, he'd be proud of how much I learned.

I smash my fists against his wrists, and his arms fall numb at his sides. I spin and thrust my stake into his chest, making impact. His eyes bulge from their sockets, but he stops me from making a kill. Surprised, I hesitate and offer him enough time to save himself.

His fist smacks into my jaw with such force, I'm certain it's broken—again. I fly backward and land in a heap on the ground several yards away. I scurry to my feet, wiping away the blood that dribbles from my mouth. I swallow down a mouthful of the thick liquid and run my tongue over my fangs. Nothing seems to be broken.

The rogue withdraws my stake and playfully spins it in his hand. Apparently I didn't account for the extra layers of muscle he has protecting his rib cage. I won't make that mistake again.

He pretends to throw the stake at me, and I flinch in response. He smiles a wide, toothy smile, and I die a little on the inside. I hate that he can bring such fear out of me even when I feel so strong.

"Did you really think this little thing would be my end?" the vampire asks. He lifts the stake and holds it loosely between two fingers.

Suddenly a quick whip of air rushes toward us. The stake is flung from the rogue's hand and is slicing through the air before landing in the hands of a witch. She uses it to stake a rogue vampire before turning to aid her fallen comrade.

While I'm happy the air witch used my weapon to eliminate a rogue, I'm slightly annoyed she left me to fend for myself. The rogue must read my thoughts on my face because he offers a sly grin before dashing toward me.

Weaponless, I have only minutes to decide my exit strategy. I can only run for so long. If I don't end this *tonight*, he will find me, and next time there really will be a missing witch—or worse.

Clenching my hands at my sides, I try to force myself to use the same magic from earlier. I don't know how to tap into it, but my odds are similar. Like earlier, I'm surrounded by rogues. Witches are dying, and my allies are weak. We're severely outnumbered, and they need me. *I* need me.

You can do this, Ava.

I have only seconds to clear my mind and search for the foreign power within me. By the time it surfaces, it's too late. The rogue is upon me.

We're thrown backward, and my head thrashes against the scratchy bark of the very tree I sent him crashing into just moments ago. Before I can stop him, the rogue thrusts his hand into my gut, using the same weak opening created earlier tonight.

I scream as I latch on to his wrist. With both hands, I fight against him. Slowly, he makes his way deeper into me. His hand is stretched, and his fingertips tease the bones of my spine. I gasp from realization.

I will never survive this.

It's now or never.

I beg the power to save me, but even though I feel it slowly sparking to life, it does not come to my aid.

Suddenly, I'm overwhelmed with anger. The fury builds within me until all I can see is red and blood and the chaos of war and death.

I *hate* this vampire. I hate everything he is, everything he stands for. I hate that his kind is the reason the witches condemned me to an eternity of loneliness. I hate that I will fight my blood lust for the rest of my life, all because I'm terrified to become something like *him*—a monster, a fiend, a ruthless and soulless waste of energy.

I sink my fingers into his flesh, and the stagnant odor of burning flesh permeates the air around me. His eyes widen, his grip loosens, and I pull him free. He's no longer inside me, but I still do not release him.

My fingers are glowing bright orange, and they're hot. The air around us becomes hazy, and that mist coats my skin. It sizzles upon impact, making this even more uncomfortable, but I refuse to stop.

I intensify my grip, grunting as I clench my jaw shut so tight, I think I hear a tooth shatter. But no, it's not *my* bones breaking. It's *his*.

He falls to his knees, and I tower over him. As I look down at him, I notice how terrified he looks. His eyes are wet with tears, and his mouth is moving. I can't hear him. I can't hear anything except for the little voice inside me that's telling me to *save myself.*

I maintain my hold on this magic until the vampire becomes so hot, his skin boils and bubbles. Just as he begins to melt into a pool of goo, his body turns to ash. He disappears before my eyes, and I walk through the rubble that was once the one vampire who haunted my dreams.

No one is fighting anymore. Everyone is watching me. I walk toward them, and the witches back away. I glance at the vampires, who are huddled around Malik, and catch my reflection in a window. Flames lick across my skin, and like a phoenix from the ashes, I rise from the shadows.

Turning my sights on the few rogue vampires who haven't retreated, I unleash my power. Just like with their former leader, they are set aflame by my mere thoughts and combust into ash before my eyes. It takes only seconds to eliminate those who were too stunned to run. I find pleasure in knowing I will hunt and kill those who evaded death today.

When the rogues are gone, I know I should force the magic down again, but I don't want to. I want to use it to rid this world of rogues once and for all, but I know if I grant it that control over my body, I will be left with nothing but a barren, lifeless planet. What's to stop it from just eliminating rogues when evil resides in all living creatures?

"Ava…"

Someone whispers my name. The voice sounds familiar, but the fear, the confusion, the disgust, does not. I turn to face her.

Mamá is before me, but she cannot stand. She's far too weak from battle. Liv and another witch are helping her walk. Together, the three lean against each other, all battered and bruised. Mamá's clothes are bloodstained and dirty with ash. Her usually tan skin is pale—maybe from her blood loss or maybe from the sight of what I've become. She doesn't hide her discomfort or the disgust she feels when she looks at me.

"*Que eres?*" she asks, her tone both queasy and weary.

"It's me, Mamá," I say softly.

The magic recoils, the flames extinguishing themselves. With the magic tucked safely back inside my body, I take a step toward her.

"No!" Mamá shouts. The witches stumble backward, trying to keep a safe distance between us.

"Just leave, Ava," Liv says. "Leave and never return."

SEVEN

I don't dare turn back as I leave Mamá's house, and I plan never to return again. They won't welcome me back after tonight's events, even though the vampires and I saved them from their doomed fate. They'll never see it that way. Not anymore. Not after witnessing what I've become.

I'd be lying if I said Liv's demeanor didn't sting. I'd hoped I could show her and the others that we're different. We're not the rogue vampires they fear. We can coexist if only they'd try to change, to see the world differently, but their turned-up noses and cast-down gazes prove they have no intention of creating a better world. In the face of such destruction, peace should be inevitable. Sadly, it's not.

We pass the gate that separates Mamá's property from the forest, and the vampires begin to run. The sun will soon rise, and we're too far from home. Amicia's manor is across town, and I know we'll never make it if we don't hurry. Already, the sky is lighter. The creatures of the night are scurrying to their beds, and the morning birds are chirping.

My skin itches from the incoming sunrise. I tingle everywhere, my heart urging me to take cover. Everything within me is screaming at me to go home, to get inside, but I cannot run. Not because I'm too weak or too tired or too sad from losing my family yet again. Something else is on my mind.

I watch the other vampires. They do not hide their joy. We won. They are celebrating with genuine smiles, heavy laughter, and high-fives. They beat death and live to fight another day. Their fear is gone, and they're giddy with adrenaline.

Sure, I'm happy too. I'm relieved to know the vampire who's been hunting me is now dust. I no longer need to look over my shoulder or expect his constant attacks. I don't need to be on edge. My friends—and former allies—aren't in danger anymore. But mostly I'm thankful because it was getting exhausting. A girl can only take so many attacks and withstand so many assaults before she breaks down. I feared for my safety and the safety of my comrades, but I don't need to anymore. My mind is at ease.

And I'm annoyed that this new sensation bubbling within me is overtaking my moment of reprieve. How often can I be happy in this world of bloodshed and chaos? The moments are few and far between, and I can't even enjoy the one time I need not fear the darkness or who may lurk there within the shadows. *Finally*, I've slain the monster, and I can't even celebrate.

The other vampires are ecstatic for our win, and I envy them. Sure, they're sad for me over my loss. They know constant rejection from one's own family is brutal psychological and emotional torture. But they truly believe in time I will forget about the witches anyway. So why not start now? Why not just move on and let them go? They don't understand. They don't have living relatives. Maybe they wouldn't be so quick to sever ties if they did.

Hikari playfully smacks Jeremiah on the shoulder. He winces. Only then do I notice the dried blood caked to his arm. Hikari doesn't as she turns to scan the woods that line our walking path. Even during recovery, the vampires seem . . . happy. Blissfully, naturally, honestly . . . happy.

As much as it pains me to do so, I can't help but question their happiness. Either vampires are incredible actors, or my friends aren't as worried as I am about the magic I used to kill the rogue vampires. Aside from initial shock, they haven't looked my way. They haven't asked me any questions. This is the second time Jasik has witnessed it, but this was the first time for the others. I expected a greater reaction from them. This magic scares the hell out of me, yet they don't seem affected. They're simply happy the fight is over and the rogue is dead. I can't help but wonder, underneath their smiles and high-fives, are they worried? Are they scared? Do they fear for my life—or theirs? Am I a danger to them? To myself?

I think I am.

What's keeping me from enjoying our victory is the innate sense that this isn't over. Something happened tonight—something that *didn't* happen last time. Using that magic to kill these rogues felt *different*. Last time, I released the magic almost as soon as I latched on to it. It was easy. It flowed through me, testing, teasing, and it willingly released me when the time came. This time, I held on too long, and I saw its teeth.

I fear this magic wants to take hold of my body and harness it as its own.

My only question is: am I strong enough to stop it?

⬖

When we reach Amicia's manor, the vampires' relaxed demeanor changes. Their happy-go-lucky attitudes morph into the terror I was already feeling. Unfortunately, this is leading us to yet another family meeting.

The parlor is dark when the shades are drawn. At the window frame's edge, a thin strip of light shines into the room. It's more than enough for my heightened senses to see the room clearly.

I can see the dust that sparkles in the air, coating it in a magical haze. There's something about the way it glitters that makes the manor feel emptier than it actually is. Thankfully, the vampires of the house have already retired for the day. They're well on their way to dreamland, and I'm left with the hunters and Amicia.

I don't feel as threatened when it's just us, even though I probably should. These five will stop at nothing to protect the vampires of this house. That's Amicia's promise to them as their sire. This is why they live in nests.

But what happens when she needs to protect them *from me*?

Holland trudges into the room, rubbing his eyes. He stretches and yawns so loudly, it makes me sleepy. I yawn too, and a still-broken rib protests by sending a stabbing pain into my gut. I grunt behind a clenched jaw. I don't want the others to see that I'm still recovering from our fight.

My body aches as bones mend, and I'm so hungry, I could drink an entire cow. My head burns, my eyes are tired, and my chest is sore. I've healed enough not to worry about things like internal bleeding and organ transplants—as if that were really an option for me—but I need a good feeding and a long day's rest before I'm back to normal.

I shift in my seat, desperately searching for but never finding a more comfortable position. My skin tingles, and I turn to find Jasik watching me, eyes concerned. Unlike the others, I don't see fear in his eyes. I see only his worry—and his devotion. I remember our almost-kiss from earlier, and my cheeks grow warm. I'm blushing, and I quickly look away.

Holland grumbles something about it being too early for him. I remember it is dawn. He lives on a human's schedule, not a vampire's. It may be late for us, but it's really early for him.

"I'm not a morning person," Holland says as he falls into the only open spot in the room save for the hardwood floor. He's sitting directly beside Jeremiah, who squirms in his seat. The two are sitting together on a small couch.

As I look around the room, I notice Hikari snickering. Jeremiah rolls his eyes in response. I find joy in their interaction because, at this very moment, no one is thinking about me or this power or how the heck we're going to fix this mess. It's like it never happened.

"I'm glad to see everyone is home safely," Amicia says. Her usual long black hair is pulled back from her face. It's shiny and sleek, like she recently oiled it. She's wearing satin pajamas. The pants trail the floor as she sweeps her legs up to sit cross-legged on the chair. She folds her hands in her lap and waits for someone to speak.

"We wouldn't have survived without Ava." Jasik says what we're all thinking. I still feel his eyes on me, but I don't glance at him.

"I assumed you would benefit from that magic again," Amicia says. She's looking at me. Her crimson eyes are void of emotion.

"How are you feeling, Ava?" Holland asks. He leans forward and rests his elbows against his knees. He's wearing pajamas as well—a plain white T-shirt and dark-blue flannel pants.

I shrug. "I'm not sure."

Holland arches a brow, his forehead creased by his concern. I don't miss how the others jostle in their seats as well. They want answers and to feel comfortable sleeping in their beds tonight.

"What do you mean?" Holland asks. His voice is soft but firm. If he has to, he will press this matter until I break.

I exhale slowly and opt for honesty. "I'm afraid this magic isn't natural."

Holland nods. "I suppose it's not, but then again, vampires aren't natural either."

"And witches are?" Jeremiah says sharply.

"Jeremiah," Amicia scolds.

He offers her a look of apology and leans back against the couch. He crosses his arms over his chest, and his leg brushes against Holland's. They both freeze. I watch this reaction as I better explain my feelings.

"What if it's not supposed to be inside me?" I say softly, eying the two carefully.

Holland's jaw clenches tightly when Jeremiah's leg rubs against his once more. I hear his breath catch. Holland squeezes his hands into balled fists and clears his throat.

"I still don't know *how* I'm doing this," I continue. Silently, I add, *Doesn't that concern anyone?* Everyone seems so comfortable and confident when we're in battle and I need to tap into this magic, but I fear we must be cautious. We still have no idea what's going on. This is new territory for everyone, including Holland, Amicia's go-to guide for all things magical.

"It doesn't seem to be hurting you," Jasik counters.

"I'm not sure it wants to hurt me," I whisper.

"What do you mean?" Malik asks. I almost forgot he was

even in the room. He has a silent way about him that makes him forgettable in the best way. I could definitely see him working as a spy for some secret government program. If he were *human*.

"What if it's trying to control me?" I ask.

The room falls silent for several breaths. It's a painful, aching silence that threatens to unnerve and bring to life my innermost secrets. The last thing I need is to live with my demons.

When Holland answers me, his eyes are tired from sleep, but I do not miss the sincerity of his words.

"Ava, I promise, I'm going to help you learn to control this magic. I won't leave until I know you're safe."

✦

After our meeting, I dash upstairs, forgoing a binge-eating session with the others in favor of solace and sleep. I'm exhausted, emotional, and way too vulnerable right now—a lousy combination for the girl who just saved the day.

Ever since I became a vampire, my life has been one nonstop ride of chaos and destruction. I haven't had much time to process and reflect. As I lean against my closed bedroom door and stare into my nearly vacant room, dressed only with items someone else had to lend me thanks to the witches who left me two whole minutes to gather my life's possessions before seeking refuge elsewhere, I take the time to consider what has become of my life.

I shower as I think, carefully washing my stomach. I've healed from my wounds, and my skin bears no mark of the truth that once existed there. Yet I feel the invisible scars as if I've been marked for life. I feel each and every time that monster assaulted my body. I shiver as I flash back to that moment—the moment he forced his hand into my core and threatened me with death. He found joy in my pain, and it sickens me that monsters like this live when so many worthy of life have died.

I think of Papá, and a knot forms in my throat. I reach for my bare chest, grazing my fingertips over the empty space between my collar bones. I haven't worn my cross necklace in two months. That's a long time to be lost.

I try not to cry, try not to focus on the monster, but my mind still wanders back to his face. The look in his eyes when he hurt me makes me happy he's dead, but now I'm left to deal with the aftermath of his destruction.

I wish I could talk to Papá. He always had a way of explaining the world to me in a way I could understand, which should be a nearly impossible feat since he was speaking to a toddler. He was robbed of the opportunity to explain it to me now, when I understand and have lived through so much more than even he ever imagined possible.

When I'm dressed in a nightgown Hikari gave me, I climb onto the massive four-poster bed and unwrap the sheer fabric, letting the sections fall naturally. Soon I'm encased in a lacy paradise and staring at my ceiling. I glance around and can see my room through the sheer fabric. I know it's not secluded, but this tiny space inside a larger room inside a manor full of vampires makes me feel safe.

I stare at the ceiling again. The fan is set to high, and each swoosh sends the little baby hairs at my crown fluttering. The rest of my hair is damp and still slick to the touch. I barely dried it before combing it with my fingers and climbing into bed. My nightgown clings to my moist skin, and the sheets are now damp. I shift uncomfortably, trying to find a dry spot on my pillow. I only succeed in dampening the entire thing, so I flip it over. The other side is cool and dry, and it eases the tension in my shoulders.

I exhale dramatically as I get comfortable and consider my situation. At seventeen, I shouldn't have the fate of our two covens on my shoulders. I still worry about Darkhaven and the humans who call it home. Now I worry about surrounding towns discovering me. Knowing I'm some sort of weird half-breed makes everything harder.

Sure, having such an insane amount of power at my fingertips feels awesome, and I love the way it envelops my entire body when I tap into it. I feel so safe, like nothing in the world can harm me, which is a pretty wicked feeling when I'm already in the midst of an epic battle.

Even so, with the rogue vampire dead, I do feel like a weight has been lifted. It feels like I can finally breathe, like I can release a breath I've been holding for months—except I had no idea I was even holding my breath. Only now, when the rogue vampire is dead, do I realize how much power he had over me.

The more I think about it, the worse I feel about myself. How did it come to that? How was I besting his minions in battle but losing an emotional war? Why did he affect me so deeply? Will every rogue who sets his sights on me make me feel this way? Or did I fear him because he stole my life from me?

I know Jasik is harboring guilt over turning me, and I haven't yet talked to him about it. He needs to know I don't blame him for his decision to finish my transition the night

I was dying. Without his help, I wouldn't have survived. I'm grateful, but I know how hard it was for him to go against everything he was brought up to believe. Amicia has strict rules about this. No vampire not sired by her is allowed refuge in her manor, yet she still allows me to stay. Is that because of her feelings for Jasik or for me?

I close my eyes and welcome darkness, banishing complex thoughts. My room is silent, as is most of the house. I hear the soft vibrations of noise somewhere far away—probably from the kitchen, where the others are celebrating another night of life. They'll refuel, and tomorrow they'll go on as if nothing happened. Meanwhile, I'll continue berating myself internally. I'll also train with Malik and study with Holland.

I cocoon myself beneath covers I don't really need but find comfort in using, and I tell myself I'm going to fall asleep as soon as I clear my thoughts. Instead, I'm staring at the ceiling fan. The blades run in circles, twirling round and round. They're passing so quickly, it looks like there's only one blade, but I know there are five.

I try to distract myself by counting them. I use my heightened senses to slow down the speed and watch as each blade passes overhead. I count to one hundred, mesmerized by the steady flow of motion and sound. Darkness creeps into the room. A wave of misty haze creeps closer and closer, until I close my eyes to it.

Later, I open them to a different place. I'm no longer lying on my bed. I'm standing in a field of wildflowers. Grass is alight with shades of yellow, purple, red, and orange. The soft smell of sweet citrus wafts toward me. The flowers smell like a strange mix of fruit and grass.

The forest is all around me. The trees are erect and do

not move even as the wind shifts. They're stiff, unnaturally unyielding, and a shiver works its way down my spine. I feel like I'm being watched. Somewhere, hidden among the trees, seeking refuge in the darkness, someone is watching me.

The tiny hairs all over my body don't literally stand on end, but they alert me nonetheless. The shift in the breeze is brushing up against something that's not supposed to be out there, and that subtle change is alerting my senses to danger.

Since I am not really here, I believe I am safe. How can my astral form be endangered? I think if I tell myself enough times that nothing can hurt me, I will believe it. Isn't that how trickery works?

Shadows from trees loom closer, moving, swaying, springing to life. The branches of a single tree sway in the breeze, and instinctively I cover my chest. Remembering the pain of my earlier assault, I suck in a sharp breath.

I know I'm not in that place anymore. The monster is forever gone. He can't hurt me again, yet I relive that moment in my mind, condemned to endless torture.

Is he here? Is he inhabiting this astral plane? I thought I sent him to hell, but what if his soul ended up here, in my dreams?

The shadows from the trees blend into one solid figure. It takes shape, growing a torso, limbs, and a head. I watch, terrified but frozen in time. I want to run, to scream, to search for help, but I cannot. I'm not in the real world anymore. I'm dreaming. I learned long ago that I cannot change what unfolds in this timeless place. I'm here to watch, to learn, to be warned. That is all. Spirit is a ruthless tyrant, and she will not be fooled by my yearning for trickery.

Even though I know I should be safe, my fear is constant

and threatening to spill from my chest. The shadow morphs into something stronger, something larger, and it begins to shift toward me. Slowly, each agonizing step closes the space between us. It moves so slowly, I'm torn between wanting to delay the inevitable and just getting it over with already.

As I watch it approach, I am mute and paralyzed in place. I choke out a muffled cry, but I know no one can hear me. I'm alone in this place save for one—the monster who has returned for me.

The shadow man is so close now. I fear I could reach out and touch him. But what would become of me? What will happen when the monster can grab on to my flesh once again? If I cannot move my flesh, I only have my mind to save me.

"I know who you are!" I shout, finding both my voice and my strength in one fell swoop.

The shadow stops, arching its faceless, black-pit head to the side. It has no eyes, no nose, no facial features at all. Its entire body is nothing but darkness, a shadow that is a constant reminder of what awaits me when death finally claims my soul. The undead don't make it to Summerland, where Papá awaits Mamá and me.

I know this is the rogue I killed. Who else would haunt my dreams? I was too confident to believe I was rid of him for good. Now, he mocks me. His shadows are slick and sleek, like the puddled goo I melted him into before he turned to ash.

"I'm not scared of you anymore," I say. I don't scream, but my voice is not soft. My words are sharp, my tone clear. If I speak only the truth, then he must believe me.

Time slows. I can hear the steady ticks of my bedside alarm clock and the slow swooshing noise from my ceiling fan. I remember I am not in a field of wildflowers, even if the grass tickles my bare feet. I am in my bedroom. I inhale deeply, hoping to sense something recognizable, but I do not smell the familiar scents of the manor. Instead, I smell flowers and weeds and an incoming rain.

The shadow beast takes another step toward me. He's so close, I can reach out and touch him, but I do not.

My arms are shaking at my sides, but I still stand tall. I want to protect myself from his attack, but I resist the urge to cover my chest with my arms. I can't let him know how he still affects me.

My lip quivers as I stare into his empty, soulless face.

He takes the final step toward me.

We now share the same breath. I hear his ragged breathing. Each inhalation crackles, and I gnaw on my lower lip to steady my racing heart. I remind myself over and over again that I'm dreaming. He cannot hurt me here. My astral self is safe on this plane, even if my mind wants to fool me.

The shadow reaches for my arm and takes my hand in his own. I do not fight him, even though I'm screaming inside. I want to stop this, to wake up, to back away, but I don't. Because that's not how this works. I am but a puppet in my mind's eye. This dream must play out as it's meant to, or it will not serve its purpose: to warn me of incoming danger.

As the shadow turns over my arm to bare my forearm, I feel a slop of bile working its way up my esophagus. I hate that he's so close, that he's touching me. It takes all of my attention not to squirm from his grasp and run through the trees. If he can seek refuge among darkness, I can too.

Suddenly the air is hot and hazy with mist. The earth beneath my bare feet is warm and moist. The soil is loose, and my toes dip into what was once firm, cold. My white nightgown is far too sheer and flows in the breeze. Sweat dribbles down my forehead and stings my eyes. I want to shake it away, but I cannot. Salty streams slide into the crevice of my mouth, and I lick my lips.

The shadow speaks to me, but I don't understand its words.

"What?" I say. My mind is foggy from the rush of the elements. All at once, they attack my vision, my voice, my hearing, my touch, my taste. I can't focus on just one thing, and it's making me nervous.

The world around me silences. I no longer hear the clock or ceiling fan. I don't hear the birds chirping or the mice scurrying. I can't hear the leaves blowing in the wind.

The same foreign words echo around me, but I know they're not coming from the shadow creature. I stare at its blank face and squint. I try to make out features, perhaps lips, but I cannot.

The shadow grips tightly to my hand, squeezing so hard, it makes my bones ache.

It speaks again. This time, there is no mistaking its words or the creature's identity.

"My will be done," she says.

A cold chill works its way down my spine. My gaze darts forward and meets her cold, steely eyes. They look just like mine—or they used to.

"Mamá?" I whisper.

A sudden flash of silver radiates across my vision, and the blade is brought down. It slices through my flesh, leaving a large crimson gash in its wake. Blood gushes from my pale skin, the wound sharp, edgy, and gaping.

I scream, engulfed in a pain so great, it feels as though this simple mark is ripping my soul from my body.

I fall to my knees and bellow until my lungs burn. Tears streak my face, and snot bubbles in my nose. My throat is coarse as I howl at the moon, for she has abandoned me when I needed her the most.

Mamá speaks, and all at once, the pain is gone, the world is silent, and I am still.

Hollow. Trapped. Dead.

EIGHT

I feel uneasy today. I woke from my dream in a sweat and had to take another shower. If I were still a witch, I would believe spirit is warning me of impending danger, but since I'm not *just* a witch, I don't know that I have access to my psyche in the same way. So far, I've only used one specific type of magic. It looks a lot like fire magic, but it feels different. Maybe I'm overthinking everything and overreacting right now. Perhaps my dream was simply a nightmare.

Before I went to bed, Holland told me we would meet in the solarium at dusk to begin our training. I'm not sure what to expect. I bet he doesn't know what to do either. I suppose we're just going to unleash the magic inside me in a controlled environment and hope for the best. Unfortunately, *the best* means not killing anyone, which means we can't work here. We need to be far away from the manor—and the vampires— before I'll feel comfortable enough to tap into my magic.

My magic.

It feels weird calling it that. Ever since I first used it while hunting with Jasik, it never felt like it was *mine*. It felt like it wasn't supposed to be part of me at all, and if Holland's right about vampire and witch mythology, then it really isn't mine. It's the part of me that should have been released into the earth when I took my final mortal breath.

The moment I woke as an immortal, I should have only had access to vampire perks. A creature with all the enhancements of a vampire—strength, speed, endurance, healing—*and* the magic of a witch is one to be reckoned with. It's freaky to think that *I* am that creature. And I used to think these hybrids only existed in books and movies.

I'm not the only one in the room. Unfortunately, I'm sharing the space with Malik, not Holland. I'd really like to leave before the house awakens. So far, every time I've had to meet with Holland, he's been late. I wonder if this is a trend I should expect from him or if he's just having trouble adapting to the vampire lifestyle. I assume he went back to a human's schedule after he and Jeremiah broke up, so I grant him leniency. It took me a while to acclimate as well.

"Don't be nervous," Malik says as he strolls over to me with mug in hand. He takes a loud slurp of his drink and sets the cup down on the table.

I was pretending to read a book I found in the parlor, but I close it now, not bothering to save my spot. Malik eyes the title curiously as he takes a seat beside me. The legs of the chair scrape against the tile floor, and I shiver. Slowly, I'm getting used to my heightened senses. These things aren't bothering me as much as they used to. Now if I can just get my emotions in check . . .

"I'm not nervous," I confirm. I paw at the book, playing with the edges. The leather cover is fraying, and it's almost impossible to read the cover text. I spin the book around in circles with my fingertips. "I just wish Holland would hurry."

"What's the rush?" Malik asks. He takes another sip of his breakfast. Unlike the rest of the house, I woke up early to feed. I wasn't sure how much I'd need to drink in order to refuel from yesterday, and it turns out, I needed *a lot*. I didn't want the other hunters to see me gobble down so much blood. I feel weak requiring so much, even if I did sustain several near-fatal injuries.

"I just want to get this day over with," I say in a huff. I realize I'm acting every bit the seventeen-year-old girl that I am, and it does annoy me to be so bratty.

Malik freezes at my outburst. He's holding his mug to his lips, but his Adam's apple hasn't bobbed. Clearly he isn't drinking. He's letting blood pool against his lips as he determines his next move.

"I guess I'm a little stressed," I say softly.

He swallows hard and swipes his tongue over his crimson-stained upper lip before answering me. "Understandable."

In this light, he looks so much like his brother. My heart leaps when I stare into his eyes and sense Jasik staring back at me. Normally when I look at them, it feels like the two couldn't be more opposite. But now, I don't think that's true.

They have the same crimson eyes all vampires have, but the shape of theirs are almost identical. They have the same nose and the same ears and the same subtle English accent that's been coated with decades of American living. Malik's voice is deeper, and his body is broader. Jasik is leanly muscled, while Malik has more bulk. I learned this the hard way during training, when he absolutely doesn't hold back. If I could bruise, I'd be a black-and-blue mess twenty-four-seven because of him.

Malik wears his hair buzzed short, while Jasik's is longer. Often he'll come down for breakfast with that just-out-of-bed tousle I'm sure he works hard for. Malik looks like he's spent his life in the military, fighting wars to honor his homeland.

I suppose he has. We are at the forefront of the war against rogue vampires in Darkhaven.

"You're going to do fine, Ava," Malik says. His words offer me comfort. I care about what he thinks of me. He's like the older brother I never had.

Immediately, I cringe at the thought. If Malik is like an older brother to me, then that would make Jasik my brother too. That bothers me more than I care to admit. I wouldn't mind Malik as a brother, but Jasik is another story. My feelings for him grow stronger by the day—and not just because he's my sire and we're irrevocably linked in a way I don't quite understand. I feel different when he's around. I feel... free.

I smile and say, "Thanks." I appreciate how hard Malik tries to make me feel comfortable around him and the other vampires. Sometimes I'm not sure if it's because he truly cares for me now that I'm a vampire or because his brother sired me. Or maybe it's because he knows something is happening between his brother and me. Regardless, I feel safe when he's around, and in a town crawling with enemies, a girl can get used to safety.

The rumbling of someone running down the stairs echoes in my mind. I lean over in my chair, getting a full view of the sitting room straight ahead. The best thing about this manor is the layout. The solarium has access to every room on the main level except for the kitchen, which means I'm never too far from anyone or out of earshot. I have to remember the latter when I'm sharing secrets.

When I was just a witch, I was always on my own. I confided in Liv and no one else. I was okay with the solitude, though. I suppose that makes me perfect for the vampire lifestyle. Aside from my nest-mates, I don't see anyone from the outside world. Living in a Victorian manor decorated with antiques, I sometimes forget what year it is.

Holland rushes down the stairs, taking the steps two at a time. He runs a hand through his hair, smoothing the ruffled layers, and scans the rooms, not taking a relaxed breath until our eyes meet.

Sorry, he mouths to me, and I smile to let him know I'm not bothered. He doesn't seem to believe me.

I think about Malik's words. Everyone is so confident I'll be okay. They all seem to believe I am strong enough to control the magic coursing in my veins.

"I'm going to do fine, huh? I guess we're going to find out," I say to Malik, finally responding to his earlier comment.

I stand and push in my chair. When I reach for the book, Malik stops me.

"I'll put it back. You stop stalling and get to training."

I roll my eyes. The ever-present protective older brother strikes again . . .

"So sorry. I overslept," Holland says when he reaches the solarium.

"It's no big deal," I say, shrugging.

"She's not lying. She likes to procrastinate on training days. Don't you, Ava?" Malik says, and I jab him in the shoulder with my elbow. He doesn't budge. Instead, he snorts at my lame attempt to injure him.

Holland laughs at our interaction before asking, "Are you ready to go, then?"

"Sure you don't need another nap?" someone says.

The three of us turn to face the intruder. Malik is once again mid-drink, and I'm tempted to tap the bottom of his mug so a little goes up his nose. Next time he'll think twice before calling me out on my procrastination habits in front of a new trainer.

Jeremiah makes his way over to us. His 'locs are pinned in place and resting atop his head. Unlike Malik, who is sporting some serious casualwear in the form of sweat pants and a T-shirt, Jeremiah is dressed for battle. I assume he's patrolling tonight, and I can't help but wonder if he requested this shift. Or am I to believe it's purely a coincidence that he is canvassing the very woods where his ex-boyfriend will be training?

When it comes to vampires, I've learned there are no coincidences. He wants to make sure his ex is safe while training with me in the middle of nowhere, and that only slightly offends me.

I don't hide the sly grin that forms, and Jeremiah doesn't miss it. He pretends not to notice, but silently I'm telling him he's fooling *no one* with his behavior. He's not over Holland, and I'm not so sure Holland is over him. I wonder if I should pry while training today. I was able to get information from Hikari before Holland even arrived, and I'm guessing Holland is *dying* to spill the beans. Who else can he talk to about his vampire ex-boyfriend besides me, the half-breed?

"I think we should go. It's getting a little *crowded* in here," Holland says. His words are sharp, but I can see straight through his tough demeanor. Beneath it all, he's hurt. Jeremiah needs to stop being such a jerk when he's around. Otherwise, he'll never win back his ex.

I didn't realize how stuffy the air inside the manor was until we get outside. It feels nice to breathe deeply and enjoy nature. It's been a long time since I have been able to stroll through the woods and not worry about someone watching me.

Unfortunately, it doesn't take long for my inner fears to

worm their way to the front of my mind.

The second we pass the wrought-iron gate that surrounds the Victorian manor, we embark upon the tree line. Darkhaven is surrounded by forest, and apparently, so are my dreams.

Correction: *nightmare.* It was a nightmare, not a dream or a vision or anything prophetic. Vampires have bad dreams too.

Even as I chastise myself internally, I think about what transpired in the dream-slash-nightmare, and I consider telling Holland. Who better to interpret them than a witch? This may be my only chance to tell him without Jasik or the other hunters eavesdropping. But if I do tell him and it turns out this is something to fear, I may get house arrest. The last thing I want to do is worry Amicia and the others. I'd also like to prevent an all-out war between the Darkhaven covens.

When the vampires find out Mamá was my assailant, they'll stop at nothing to eliminate the threat once and for all. While I'm not fond of the witches at the moment, I don't hold grudges. I'll get over their treatment eventually, and I think it would just be easier if we all lived separate lives and stayed out of each other's way.

"Penny for your thoughts?" Holland says, breaking the silence.

"Hmm?" I say, even though I heard him.

"You seem lost in your mind. Anything you want to talk about?"

He shoves his hands into his pockets and shivers. He holds his arms close against his body as he exhales puffs of lacy steam. Being a vampire, I forget how cold the world can be to a mortal. I feel guilty for insisting we train outside the manor. Holland didn't protest, but I still pressed it. I didn't want to harm the vampires, but in doing so, I condemned Holland to spend *hours* in the cold dark of night.

"Will it be too cold for you out here?" I ask. Holland is thin and short. He's only a couple inches taller than me. He pales in comparison to Jeremiah's height and build. Holland looks frail beside his ex.

When the wind blows, his hair ruffles and his nose turns pink. I don't think he would notice the color change if he looked at himself in a mirror, but I can see it clearly. I can practically hear the blood rushing from his nose to other parts of his body. Every time the constricted vessels dilate, a brief burst of blood causes his nose to turn from light pink to bright red. I lick my lips at the thought of it.

"No, and don't change the subject." He winks at me as he releases the tension in his shoulders. His arms fall more naturally to his sides, like he's trying to prove he can compete with the vampires even when it's so cold out. He doesn't fool me. His hands are balled into fists, and his skin is pale white.

"I'm not. I just—"

"I'm fine, Ava. Now tell me what you were thinking about," Holland says, growing more irritated with me.

I groan internally. "Why does it matter?"

"Because you were deep in thought," he says. "I bet it was important."

"How do you know?" I ask, still stalling.

"Because I've been talking since we left the manor, and you haven't even heard me, have you?" he asks.

He's right. I haven't. I had no idea he said a word, but I lie. "Sure I did."

Holland stops abruptly and turns to face me. He crosses his arms over his chest—in a show of defiance or for warmth, I'm not sure. "Prove it."

"Prove it? How?" I ask. I know what he's going to say, but I ask anyway.

"Tell me what I said."

I grumble incoherently before speaking up. "Fine, okay? I didn't hear you. I wasn't listening. I was too worried about your comfort. My bad."

Holland rolls his eyes. "Lies. Tell me what's on your mind."

I don't answer right away. Holland is making it clear that he won't budge on the matter. Either I can tell him what I was thinking about or we will sit out here all night until he freezes to death. Sadly, I'm not sadistic enough for the latter, but I kind of wish I were. I resolved this already. *It was a nightmare.*

"I had a bad dream." I shrug. "That's all."

Holland arches a brow, clearly interested. "What kind of dream?"

I relent and say, "A vision ... *Maybe.*"

"Well, my interest is piqued. Tell me about it."

I summarize the dream as best I can and wait for his response.

"Ava, this doesn't sound good." Holland speaks softly, like he's trying to calm a wild animal or coax a friend from a ledge. I don't like his tone at all.

"I know," I admit.

"Are you going to tell the others?"

I shrug. "How do I know it's not *just a dream*."

"You know, Ava. *You know.*" He emphasizes the last two words by pausing slightly.

I shake my head. "I'm not a spirit witch anymore, Holland. This is literally *impossible.*"

"How can you say that? How can you even *believe* that? Is it possible to be this stubborn?" Holland is shouting now, and it makes me uncomfortable.

Suddenly I'm aware of how far we are from home. We're isolated, lost in the woods where so few venture. Even so, I was attacked in these very woods by creatures who were sent to kill me. I can't shake that feeling, even if I know their leader is dead.

"Just . . . stop. Calm down," I say, scanning the surrounding trees.

"What is it?" Holland asks. He steps closer, nearly closing the space between us. His arm brushes against mine as we both stare into the darkness. Unfortunately, he can't see anything, but I can. I see endless rows of trees and brush and shadows. Enemies can be hiding *anywhere*.

"This was stupid. We're too far. We should head back," I say.

"But you're the one who wanted to go into the woods," Holland says cautiously. "I've been following your lead."

I swallow the knot that forms in my throat. "I'm not sure I'm ready for this, Holland."

"For what? Training?"

"For all of this. This is all just too much. First the rogues, then the magic, and now dreams. Every time I think I have the upper hand, I'm reminded of just how mortal I truly am."

Holland smiles softly. "Vampires are always described as immortal creatures, but that's just because you're so different from the rest of us. But you're not indestructible, Ava. You have to accept that there are dangers in this world that will come for you, especially now that we know you're . . . different."

I shake my head. "I didn't expect to be limitless when I transitioned, but I certainly thought I wasn't going to be bogged down by the witches and their baggage. I feel cursed, Holland!"

Holland reaches for me, but I pull away. I can see I've hurt him by the look in his eyes, but I don't care.

"Ava, you're not cursed. You're special. Sometimes, being special, being *different*, can feel like a curse, but it's not. You're *not* cursed."

"I—I don't want to talk about this anymore. I just… I need some time alone. Can you get back okay?"

"I—uh…" Holland scans our surroundings, finding his bearings. "I guess. I think so."

I don't wait for him to ask me to stay, because I know he will. I also know I will falter. I will stay and help him get back, but right now I need some serious me time. I need space.

The second Holland tells me he's okay, I vanish. I run full speed as far as I can. I don't know where I'm running, and I don't care. I just run until my legs ache and the ground disappears.

✦

My legs are dangling over the ledge of a steep cliff when I hear him approach. I don't need to face him to know he's there. I *feel* him. I sense him in a way I don't sense others. He feels it too, this invisible link that tethers us together for all eternity. It's there, even now and even when he's miles away. I always feel him.

I don't turn around. Instead, I stare into the abyss of forest. It offers seclusion rarely granted to picturesque towns not in television shows. We get the occasional tourist, but we aren't bombarded like most places. I feel lucky to have grown up here, surrounded by nature. That's important to witches and, apparently, to vampires as well.

The stars are bright in the sky above me. They twinkle and reflect off the still water. They dance across waves and splash at the rocky banks below. The water is clear. It's so clear, I can see the sand below. The deeper the water, the darker the depths. I used to swim here and try to hold my breath until I swam all the way to the bottom. I was young and certain there were treasures below where no one had gone before. Unfortunately, I never reached what lies below. I didn't have the lung capacity for such a feat. I think I do now, yet I don't wish to jump in. I like not knowing the sea's secrets. I can respect there are some things that need not be discussed.

Jasik sits down beside me. Our legs brush together. My skin tingles where our bodies connect. Even through layers of clothing, I can feel the sensation growing. My heart flutters when he's so close to me. I like the way it feels, but I don't care for it much. It makes my head foggy and my speech gibberish.

"How'd you find me?" I ask quietly. The waves are crashing against the rocks below. The salty air tingles my nose, and I scrunch to avoid a sneeze. The air is misty with an incoming rain. I can smell it. It is a fresh earthy scent, like musk and grass mixed together. I love it.

Jasik is silent for a moment before speaking. When he does answer me, he glances over. I can feel his eyes on me, but I don't budge. I wait for his answer.

"Even if I were blind, I could find you."

His voice is a whisper, and his words pierce my heart. My breath catches in my throat, and I finally face him. His eyes sparkle in the moonlight. When he looks at me, his crimson irises change. They're bolder, brighter, turning neon and glowing.

"Jasik…" I speak softly, but I don't really say anything

at all. I'm not sure I need to. He can understand my meaning from one simple word. I'm sure of this.

"Holland told me what happened. He worries you fear you're cursed. This can't be true... Is it?" Jasik asks.

I look away. I can't stare into his eyes and admit my deepest insecurities when he's looking so annoyingly and breathtakingly perfect.

"You don't know what it's like to be a freak." My voice is raspy with emotion.

"Ava..."

Jasik whispers my name and tucks loose strands of hair behind my ears. He repeats the motion when the wind blows them free again. Self-consciously, I run a hand over my hairline, desperately trying to apply enough pressure to keep my frizz from fluttering in the breeze. I know it's a lost cause, but I can't stop myself.

"Why can't you see how extraordinary you are?" he asks.

A knot forms in my throat. I face him again, and our feet interlock. I wrap my ankle around his and lean toward him.

"You think I'm extraordinary?"

"I think you're radiant."

I smile and drag my teeth against my lower lip. "You think I'm radiant?"

"I think you're bewitching, Miss López."

We both laugh at the double meaning. I lean against Jasik and rest my head on his shoulder. Together we watch the moon dance across the water and the stars shoot across the sky.

We don't speak, not even when we begin to breathe in unison. As the seconds tick closer to sunrise, we sit, transfixed by the feeling of our souls intertwining.

Jasik turns his hand to reveal his palm, and I slide my

hand into his. Our fingers thread together, and I feel as though life can't possibly get more perfect.

In the back of my mind, I know I've disappointed Holland and probably Malik too. Now that I'm not an emotional wreck, I'm ready to face this problem head-on, because Jasik is right.

I am extraordinary, and it's time this magic inside me submits to *me*.

❖

Something slams into me with such sharp force, it steals my breath, and my lungs ache from the sudden exhalation. My limbs flail uncontrollably as I try to steady myself. My head lulls to the side as my body is catapulted from where I was standing. The strain on my shoulders stings at my muscles, and sharp needle pains stab at the base of my skull.

My vision is blurry. I see flashes of light. I think I see multiple figures standing in the distance, but I can't be sure. My senses are in overdrive, and I can't focus on any one thing. All I know is I'm flying through the air now, body limp.

I tumble to the ground in a heap, rolling until I finally skid to a stop. I'm on my back, staring at the starlit sky, and I take my first full breath since the attack. I suck in a breath so forcefully, I nearly choke on it. The quick burst of air tickles the back of my throat, and I cough, rolling onto my side until my lungs finish spasming.

Get up, Ava. Get up and fight.

I roll onto my stomach, and by the time I'm crouched on all fours, I finally stop hacking. I sit up, resting my bottom on the heels of my feet and my hands on my thighs. I'm breathing heavily as I scan my surroundings.

I blink away tears, a natural reflex from choking, as I stare into the eyes of my friends.

Hikari, Jeremiah, Malik, Jasik, and even Holland are standing several yards away, watching me as I rise.

"What the he—"

"This is an important lesson, Ava," Malik says, interrupting me. His tone is harsh, and I'm certain he's annoyed with me because of what happened earlier with Holland.

"What lesson is that, Malik? How to fall?" Jasik says. He doesn't hide his irritation.

Jasik is at my side as I stand but still offers his hand as aid. I wave him away, not wanting to look weak in front of the others. I'm embarrassed to know they've already caught me by surprise. Every time I think I'm gaining Malik's trust, something happens to derail my efforts. At this rate, he may never end our training sessions.

"You must always be prepared," Malik says. "Enemies are everywhere."

"Yeah, apparently they're even residing within my own home," I say, frustrated. I brush away the loose dirt from my hands and saunter toward the others.

My body aches from the landing, not from the impact of the initial blow. Whoever attacked me truly must not have wanted to harm me—just teach me a lesson. By the coy smile on Hikari's face, I'm guessing she was my assailant. She swoops her messy bangs to the side and playfully winks at me. It's hard to stay mad at the vampires when I know they're just trying to teach me how to survive.

"You were distracted, and you believed you were safe," Malik says.

I grumble something under my breath about how I *should*

be safe when I'm on my own property, which only irritates Malik. I need to learn to bite my tongue, because I will surely pay for my attitude later. And I thought my body was sore *now*.

"Just because the rogue is dead does not mean you are safe from danger, Ava—regardless of where you are," Malik says. "Never forget that."

I nod, not just because I want this lesson to be over but because he's right. The rogue may be dead, but I'm never out of danger. I should have learned that from the many battles I've fought during the course of my short life. Last night's dream should serve as a reminder as well.

I can't trust anyone—not even my own blood.

NINE

I want to apologize, but I can't find the right words. Saying "I'm sorry I abandoned you in freezing weather in the middle of woods that might have been overrun with rogue vampires" just doesn't seem to convey the right amount of regret.

"It's okay," Holland says, reading my mind. He smiles at me and seems generally unaffected by my betrayal. "I know newborns are ornery. It takes a while to get used to all those emotions." He winks.

"I *am* sorry," I say. I hope my tone reflects my honesty. Holland and I may not be actual friends yet, but what I did was a crappy thing to do, even if I was overwhelmed by my emotions. It's getting easier to control them, but in the meantime, I have to try not to ruin all my relationships.

"I know," he says, nodding.

"It won't happen again," I add. I'm babbling now, but I can't stop myself.

"Don't get ahead of yourself," he says with a chuckle. "You've got a long way to go before you shed your newborn status."

"Is that why you set up the attack? To teach me a lesson?" My words are harsher than intended. Honestly, I am just curious. I try to convey that I'm not upset with Holland for telling the others about my mental breakdown by smiling. The moment comes across as insincere, and I have a feeling I look like a psycho.

I watched a documentary about Ted Bundy, one of the most notorious serial killers I'm familiar with, and I'm pretty sure I look just like he did when he was in court, dressed in prison garments and handcuffed at his hands and feet, and still smiling and waving at the cameras who were filming his trial. *Awkward.*

Holland stares plainly before answering. "No, it was Malik's idea. Hikari was happy to help him with his, uh, *lesson.*"

I knew it!

I snort. "I'm not surprised. Malik has no faith in me." Again, my tone is hard. I gnaw on my lower lip. The last thing I want is for Holland to think I'm a jerk and refuse to help me. I need to learn how to sound less cranky.

"He only wants what's best for you," Holland says, defending Malik, my ruthless trainer. I like how easy it is for him to defend a vampire. I wish it was like this for everyone. Life would be a lot easier if it were just vampires and witches versus rogues—and not the way it is now. Too much unnecessary bloodshed has wreaked havoc on the species, but there can be peace. The witches just have to want it.

I kick at the sticks on the ground and relish how they crunch under my weight. When they snap, I feel it in my head and limbs and even in my heart. I thought being a vampire was a death sentence, but now I'm not so sure. Having heightened senses has allowed me to experience the world differently, and I love it.

"Yeah, I know, but it sucks sometimes. I just wish Malik believed in me. I always feel like such a disappointment to him," I say, shrugging. It's weird being vulnerable with someone I barely know. I want to ask Holland questions about his life, but I don't. I'm not sure he's ready yet. I need to wait for the right moment to let him know he can lean on me too. We're both witches—*sort of*—living in a house full of vampires. Who better to talk to about life's quarrels?

At this, Holland arches a brow and looks generally confused. "You're kidding, right?"

"What do you mean?" I ask. I push aside brush so Holland can easily pass through, and then I follow behind him. I'm not sure where we're going, so I let him take the lead. The walking trail is narrow, so we walk single file as we chat.

"In all the years I've known these vampires, Malik has *never* offered to train someone. In fact, he regularly turned away those who wanted to learn from him. The fact that he's working with you now—regardless of how this all started—means he definitely believes in your potential." Holland talks with his hands as we walk, and I see them poking out at his sides every few words.

I'm silent while I consider his words. "I guess... I guess I've never thought of it like that." Knowing Malik *does* trust in my former training puts a smile on my face. All this time, I thought he felt obligated to train me because of what his brother did, but that's not the case. He's doing this *for me*. It seems Malik is familiar with more emotions than I give him credit for.

"You have to stop being so hard on yourself, Ava," Holland says.

We reach a fork in the path, and Holland guides us to the right. This must be an official hiking trail in the forest, because we're no longer trudging through layers of brush and decay. The walkway is dirt with only a few stones and broken branches in our way. Wide enough to fit us both side by side, the route is bordered by bushes, and endless rows of trees lie beyond that.

"I'm working on it," I say.

What I don't admit to is how hard it is for me to relax. Growing up with Mamá after Papá died wasn't always easy. She was relentless in her pursuit of making me the best witch I could be. She wanted me to become high priestess of our coven one day, and because of that, our relationship came second to the coven.

Growing up, I was okay with that. I assumed that was how it was in all covens. Then I met Liv, whose coven desired peace, not violence. I used to think they were crazy, that there was no rationalizing with vampires. Now I see they were right all along. It sickens me to know I forced Liv into fights, because she's a different person now. I did that to her. I made her a monster, a murderer.

"I know Malik is hard to read. He's not emotional like the rest of us," Holland says, cutting into my thoughts. He chuckles. "But it's obvious he cares for you, and to care about someone, you have to believe in them."

I nod. "I know. He's not as impassive as he likes people to think."

"Yeah, he's a big softy under all that muscle."

We both laugh, and it feels good to relax a little. The friendship growing between us was off to a rocky start, but I don't think Holland will be leaving the manor anytime soon. It's important to me that we're on good terms—and not just because he's the only witch who doesn't look at me like I'm an abomination. I actually do like him, and I can sense his loneliness. It's not easy being a witch without a coven, but it's not easy being a witch *in* a coven either. I never realized witches had it so bad ...

"In all seriousness, I'm glad Jasik found you and convinced you to come back," Holland says.

"Yeah, he's pretty spectacular like that," I say softly.

"*Spectacular*, huh?" Holland offers a wide, toothy smile and wiggles his eyebrows at me. His grin is all-knowing, and I feign overdramatic discomfort. I swat his shoulder and pretend he's being ridiculous, but inside I'm screaming. It's been a long time since I've been able to sit around and talk about boys. The last time I did this, I was living an entirely different life. And I was with Liv. I'd be lying if I said her last words to me didn't sting. I never thought my best friend would tell me to never return to the place I once called home.

We walk in silence for several minutes while I find the courage to mention the one thing I really don't want to talk about. But I know I have to.

"Holland, do you think my dream was a premonition?"

I hold my breath while waiting for his response. Only now do I realize how much this does bother me. I'm terrified he'll say yes, because that means I have bigger problems than I can sanely handle. But at the same time, I'm not sure I want him to say no. While I have severed ties with the witches, their ancestry is still part of me. Before I used magic to save Jasik and myself, I thought I'd never again be able to honor that heritage. Maybe I was wrong.

"I'm not sure, but if I've learned anything, it's that we need to assume the worst—"

"And hope for the best?" I say, interjecting. I think this may be the single most annoying phrase of all time.

He smiles. "Exactly. The good news is, if it wasn't just

a dream, we've been warned that the witches may be up to something naughty."

I exhale sharply. "When are they *not* up to something bad?"

"Yeah . . . right?" Holland's eyes are glossy, and I know that look. He's reminiscing about earlier times. He doesn't have to tell me he's picturing his former coven. I've been away from mine long enough to know that's exactly what a witch thinks about when he's on the verge of homelessness. My heart aches for him because I understand his pain. Betrayal from the home is the kind of pain time can never mend.

"Do you want to talk about it?" I ask.

Holland blinks several times, and his eyes clear. He's back to reality. "Talk about what? Your dream?"

I know he's trying to change the subject. He knows I'm not talking about my dream. I consider giving him his space and the time he needs to confront his demons, but I press on.

"Why did you leave your coven?" I ask.

Holland slouches and hunches over as he walks, playing with the dead grass at his feet. His hands are shoved into his pockets, and he's staring at the ground. I realize how much smaller he looks when we're hiking in a massive forest. Or maybe he just shrinks when he thinks about his former life. I know I do.

After several minutes of silence, he shrugs and says, "I'm just different, I guess. I didn't buy into the us-versus-them mentality, and eventually my coven became resentful."

"You thought there could be peace," I say. It's not a question. I already know the answer. Sadly, a lot of vampires died at my hands because I was too stubborn to consider the possibility that the witches have been lying to me about a lot of things for a very long time. Until I became a vampire myself, it never occurred to me that friendships could be formed between the two species.

Holland nods. "I did. No one else wanted that, so I was forced to leave."

I reach over and link my arm through his. Holding on to him firmly, I say, "I'm so sorry, Holland. Betrayal by one's family is a difficult cross to bear."

"Only the strong and the willful know this to be true," he says.

He withdraws his hand from his pockets and holds my hand. Our palms touch, and sparks shoot through my skin and up my arm. He interlocks his fingers with mine but doesn't speak. We walk like this for a long time. The tingling sensation of mortal flesh against my own never wanes, but slowly it becomes easier to resist the urge to squeeze his hand so tightly that blood vessels rupture and bones snap.

"We're almost there," Holland says.

I inhale sharply. It's a loud echo in the silent forest, and I know Holland hears it.

"You're going to get through this, Ava. I have a feeling you're stronger than we can even imagine."

"The strength is the worst part," I say, pulling my hand free from his grasp. I cross my arms over my chest and squeeze tightly. It's painful, but it gives me something to focus on besides the reason we're in the woods in the first place.

"I know it's not easy, but if anyone can do this, it's you."

"How can you be so sure? How do you know I'm strong enough?" I ask.

"Because I've met you."

✦

"You're tense. You need to relax," Holland says. I watch as he moves his torso, stretching his core muscles. He cracks his neck and twists his spine. He hunches his shoulders forward and back and then forward again. As he moves, I hear faint cracks from his joints.

I mimic him and try to clear my mind. I can't help but be on edge. We're sitting in the middle of a field of wildflowers. The forest surrounds us, and all I can think about is my dream.

When we got here, I froze. This location is eerily similar to the one in my dream, and he told me he chose this location for that reason. I need to be the one in control; the dream cannot be in control of me. How better to accomplish this than by fighting my fear head-on? So we practice magic in the very place that haunts my dreams.

"How do you feel?" Holland asks. "Better?"

I think before answering, surprised by my own words. "Actually, yes. A little."

Holland smiles. "Good. Close your eyes and try to clear your mind."

I do as he instructs, but after too many seconds pass in silence, I peek. Holland is staring at me, a disappointed glare piercing his face.

"Ava," he says in a voice that betrays his annoyance. "We will never finish before the sun rises if you don't take this seriously."

"I know. I'm sorry. It's just…this place gives me the heebie-jeebies," I say. I scan the forest for the hundredth time. Again, I find nothing out of the ordinary. The shadows are the same ones that are always there. They have yet to morph into something more sinister, like my knife-wielding mother.

"It shouldn't," Holland says. "You were born a witch and reborn a vampire. You come from nature, and if you want to harness its power, you must become one with it."

"How very Zen of you," I say. Internally, I laugh at my joke, but externally, my features don't budge. The last thing I want to do is annoy him further. I'm already on thin ice, and if he decides to cancel training, I'll have no one to turn to but the vampires. And I can't risk their lives.

He groans and rolls his eyes. "You have to take this seriously."

"I am," I argue. I'm defensive, but I shouldn't be. I know he's right.

He gives me a pointed look, so I try to better convince him.

"I promise I'll concentrate," I say.

He exhales slowly but loudly, and I understand his double meaning. "So, I'm thinking this is similar to witch magic. First you need to focus, and then you need to tap into it. We'll start slow today, but I think you already have the tools to excel. You were born a witch and harnessed spirit magic. This shouldn't be any different."

I nod. "I guess."

"Now, close your eyes and clear your mind," Holland instructs. "We need to meditate."

Instinctively, I focus on my breath. With each inhalation, my lungs expand and my chest fills. When I exhale, I listen to the soft thumps of my heart. It still surprises me that I have a heartbeat. Then again, I thought vampires were monsters, and monsters aren't supposed to be so ... *mundane.* I dig deeper and listen to my body. My muscles stretch when I move. I sway from side to side, never breaking my meditative state.

Once I'm comfortable with the sounds of my own body, I move on to Holland's. His heart thuds loudly in his chest. His breath comes in short, shallow bursts. There's a quiet swooshing sound as blood courses through his veins. Sometimes when we're together, I forget he's mortal. I forget his life force is the one thing I require to survive. My stomach grumbles, but I ignore the desire to feed. The more time I spend with Holland, the easier it is to resist the urge to feed. Soon, I'll be able to venture into town and not kill anyone.

I expand my senses to the trees and the flatland we're utilizing for today's lesson. I listen as wildlife scurries through the brush. The sound of life is precious to my ears. I love listening to owls in the sky and wolves on the ground. Suddenly I'm overwhelmed with the pain of knowing I'll never see another sunrise or listen to songbirds chirp. How do vampires live an eternity without these things?

"Remain focused," Holland whispers, as if he can read my mind. I know he can't. My face likely betrays that I've gone off course and need to be guided back. I make a mental note to tell Holland he's a pretty good teacher and should consider forming his own coven.

I sink further into the abyss, listening to sounds that resonate from miles away. I can hear the sea. Waves crash against rocks, and fish flutter through the water. I hear distinct voices, but they're quiet, barely audible. I ignore the speakers and retract my senses. I don't want to be so far away. I need to focus on me—or rather, on what's *inside* me.

I focus on the essence burning within me. It shines brightly, an iridescent energy source that's practically begging to be tapped into. It swirls in circles within my core. I sense that it is powerful, formidable, and beautiful. The longer I focus on it, the larger it grows. Slowly, it moves, spreading throughout my body, seeping into every crevice of my being.

I want to touch it, but I don't know how. I don't know if I should. I remember that Holland is here, and he will help to keep me safe if anything should happen. It's now or never.

Internally, with my own essence, I probe the magic inside me. It is dazzling, defiant, and dominant. This magic is everything I want to become as I transition into my vampire life. I want to be strong and powerful, just like this magic.

As the iridescent glow completely fills me, I begin pulling at it, tugging it outward. In a quick burst, I throw back my head, grinding my teeth, and the shimmery glow within me seeps from my aura. I open my eyes, staring in awe as it surrounds me completely. I sit within a protective bubble, giggling as Holland reaches to touch it.

As his fingers lightly dance across the outer layer of my magic, I laugh. "That tickles."

"Ava, this . . . this is incredible!"

"It feels even better," I say softly.

"It's so many colors. I see white and blue and green and red and purple," Holland says. He's breathing heavily and still palming the magic surrounding me.

"I'm going to try something," I say, but I don't commit until Holland nods. He withdraws his hand and waits for me to continue.

Focusing on the witch before me, I expel the magic, pushing it away from me and closer to him. At an agonizing pace, the magic seeps toward him, until it glides right against his body. He smiles as it surrounds him, pulling him inside to join me. Together, we laugh and enjoy the feeling of the energy source I've feared since the very first time I used it.

When the magic recedes back into my body, I'm still giddy with energy, but I feel different. I'm not scared of it anymore. It doesn't feel like it wants to consume me. In fact, it feels like it's *part* of me. For so long, I thought this magic inside me wasn't supposed to be there. Like I was damaged goods or a broken vampire or something. But now I think it was supposed to be there all along. I guess this is one of the perks of being a spirit witch who's turned into a vampire. And I have to admit, I rather like this perk.

I jump forward and envelop Holland in a tight hug. Freezing in place, he flinches as my arms wrap around him. I know I've startled him, but I don't release him from the hug until he relaxes in my arms. Only then do I pull away.

"Thank you, Holland. This is the first time I've felt . . . safe and strong."

My words spill out of me before I have a chance to consider them. I'm baffled by my confession. I stare at my hands as I think about what I just said. Of course I feel safe around the vampires, but not like this. This is different. Finally I feel safe in my own skin. I have been terrified for so long. I feared what I was, what I could do. But now I know it's just a matter of time until I can control this magic and use it for good.

❖

When we finally return home, I'm feeling better about the power growing inside me. I know I have a long way to go, but with practice and Holland's help, I know I can control it. And once I do, rogues won't stand a chance. I try not to get ahead of myself, though. That kind of strength will probably take years to harness. Thankfully, I have that kind of time.

I take the steps toward the front door two at a time and pat the gargoyle on the head as I enter. This has become ritual for me. I once read gargoyles protect where they're guarding, so the last thing I want to do is upset the little guy. With witches hell-bent on ruining my dreams, we need all the protection we can get.

Holland and I enter the foyer together and shout to the others that we're back. Conveniently, Jasik and Malik are already expecting our return.

"Is Jeremiah still patrolling?" I ask as I walk into the parlor. I don't miss how Holland's heart races at the sound of his ex-lover's name.

"Yeah," Jasik says.

"How was training?" Malik asks.

The two are sitting at the tiny table positioned directly in front of the large bay windows in the parlor. Resting on the tabletop is years' worth of dust. Malik is staring at the chessboard with an intense glare in his eyes, while Jasik is sitting back in his chair, the heel of his right foot resting against his left thigh. He's smiling brightly and strumming his fingertips against the table, urging Malik to make a move.

Jasik glances at me and lifts his brows. It seems Malik is determined to give the chess game another chance, but he's clearly desperate to avoid losing to his little brother.

Holland and I take a seat on the couch across from the two and watch them play. After several minutes, Malik throws his arms in the air and announces that he hates this game.

Laughing, I say, "So who wants to hear about my terrific training session?"

This gets both of their attention.

"Wait for me!" Hikari calls from another room. She walks in from the solarium with a mug of blood in hand. She takes a loud slurp as she takes a seat in a chair beside the fireplace. Her pixie-cut hair is messy, with her bangs pushed to one side. "Now that these two are done with this stupid game, I can come back into this room without losing my mind."

"The game's not over yet," Malik says. He's annoyed, and his voice betrays that.

Hikari groans loudly. "Ugh! Seriously?"

"It's time to admit defeat, brother," Jasik says. He still has a stupid grin slapped across his face, so I can imagine why Malik is irritated with everyone.

Malik tosses Jasik a look that tells him he will never admit defeat, and then he looks at me. "Let's talk about training."

"What? Malik wants to talk about training? No surprise there," I say with a chuckle.

Holland and I update the hunters, describing everything that happened. Talking about it is almost as incredible as experiencing it. But being vampires, the hunters don't understand what it's like to connect so deeply with yourself, and that saddens me. Since they can't comprehend magic, they focus on the technical issues. And that's a major joy kill.

"What if Holland was a vampire? Would it have the same effect?" Jasik asks.

Jasik's lack of enthusiasm, while expected, is upsetting. I want more from my sire. I want him to be as excited about this as I am. But I give him the benefit of at least thinking about his question before I answer.

Finally, I say, "I don't know. I guess we'd have to try and see."

"Yeah," Holland says with a loud laugh. "Any volunteers?"

"Maybe I should practice some more before we jump into the big stuff, like controlling the magic and not killing everyone."

"It'll only be a matter of time before you're able to call upon the magic and use it at your discretion," Holland says.

"So, basically, everything is still the same? You just feel better about it now?" Hikari says.

"Hikari," Jasik says sharply.

"I'm serious," she says. "Basically you can still only use it if you're in trouble, and even then, you may not be able to control how much you use?"

I nod. "I need more time, guys. But yes, I haven't mastered it yet, so we have to be careful."

The front door opens, and Jeremiah strolls in, scanning the room until his gaze lands on Holland. He stiffens slightly, standing straighter, and I hear the nearly silent sharp inhalation that betrays his innermost desires. The other vampires pretend not to notice.

"How was patrol?" Jasik asks. He eyes me cautiously, as if silently telling me not to mention what we all just heard. It's times like these when I wish Holland was a vampire. He would have heard Jeremiah and realized they feel the same way. If only *someone* would speak up, these two lovebirds would be back together already. I still don't know what separated them, but I bet it can be resolved with simple communication.

Jeremiah shrugs and takes the open seat directly across from Holland. "Uneventful."

This catches my attention. It's interesting that the other vampires and witches of Darkhaven are keeping to themselves. In a town crawling with supernaturals, there is never an uneventful night. Rogue vampires hunt nightly, so where are they?

"You didn't see anything at all?" I ask.

Jeremiah shakes his head. "Just humans in town."

I arch a brow. "You went that far?"

"Well, the woods are empty, so I checked on the witches and then went into town."

"And you didn't see anything strange?" Malik asks. Clearly our training sessions are causing us to be on the same wavelength. We both find this odd.

"I said no already," Jeremiah says, his voice tinged with annoyance.

"What is it?" Jasik asks.

"It's just . . . strange that the witches *and* rogues took the same night off," I say. "That almost never happens."

"Well, your coven was just attacked," Hikari says. "They're busy with the aftermath."

I groan internally. I wish she would stop calling them *my coven*. They're not my coven anymore. I don't comment on it, choosing to remain focused on the issue at hand, but I hope she can sense my frustration.

"Sure, but what about the rogues? We didn't fight every rogue nearby, and some did escape. Where are they?"

"Ava, I'm sure it's nothing," Jasik says. His voice is soft, calm, soothing, but it irritates me.

"If I've learned nothing else since becoming a vampire, I know there is no such thing as a coincidence."

Something is coming, and I will be ready for it.

TEN

It's been twenty-four hours since I tapped into my magic, and I'm itching to connect again. Unfortunately, it's my turn to patrol. Jasik argued I should get a pass since training with Holland is more important, but I could tell the others needed a break. Even Holland seemed excited to spend the evening confined to the manor with the vampires—*and his ex.*

I have to admit, I'm way more interested in Holland's former relationship and his past life with his coven than I thought I would be. When he first arrived, I only cared to understand why a house of vampires was calling on a witch for help. That seemed odd and something I've never experienced in my time as a witch. I was intrigued, and I wanted to make sure I knew what I was getting into.

Now, I can tell these two lovebirds want to rekindle their romance, but Jeremiah is too stubborn and Holland is too scared to reconcile. We may be immortal, but that doesn't mean we're invincible. Death will catch us one day, so life is too short to hold grudges when you're in love.

Jasik wants me to butt out. He hasn't actually said those words, but he doesn't need to. I can practically read his mind at this point. He gives me one stare, and I know exactly what he's thinking. It's terrifying but still exciting that I can connect with someone on such a deep level. Since I'm basically an orphan now, it's nice to have a friend—or whatever we are.

I glance at Jasik, who's patrolling with me tonight. The others still don't believe I can be trusted to hunt alone. Sure, they let me off my leash every once in a while, and during those times, I run free and wild like a mangy mutt. I don't return home until the sunlight is licking my heels. That's probably why they fear for my safety. I take too many risks for these old vampires. They're set in their ways, and they need someone young and fresh to show them the world is pretty incredible if only they would leave the manor.

In years past, I've never felt the desire to leave Darkhaven. I knew it was my responsibility to keep the town safe, but now that I've *sort of* severed that responsibility, I can travel, see the world, experience other cultures, meet new people… The possibilities of this new life are endless and exciting.

Jasik must feel my eyes on him, because he turns to face me. Quickly, I look away, but I know I'm not fast enough. He catches me gawking, and now I'm fighting back a smile. I love the way he makes me feel, and I hope that never changes.

I look up at the sky. Another full moon will soon be upon us. Time is moving so quickly, I can barely keep up with all these changes. I'm starting to enjoy my time as a vampire, and I don't regret my choice and Jasik's decision to turn me. Amicia even seems to count on me. I feel like I'm a valued member of a team, and as strange as it sounds, I've never felt that way before. The witches work similarly to the vampires, but I always felt like an outcast. I don't anymore, and that's pretty awesome.

The night sky twinkles overhead. The stars and moon are bright enough to light the forest as we walk silently. Jasik is close enough to touch. Every few steps, the back of my hand grazes the back of his, and sparks ignite in my soul.

Whenever I'm around my sire, I feel a roller coaster of emotions. Sometimes being around him is so intense, I can barely breathe. Other times, I relish in the calmness of it. Jasik makes me feel safe, wanted, desired ... Ever since I first transitioned, I've known Jasik will always be by my side. I'm not sure I can navigate this chaotic life without him, so I'm glad to know I mean as much to him as he means to me.

I used to worry my feelings were because of our sire bond. At first I was wary of it. I didn't want him to control me. I'd just freed myself from the witches, and all they wanted to do was dominate me. Mamá controlled every part of my life, and I was too naïve to question if it *should* be that way or if I should have more of a say. I was so used to it, I spent my nights risking my own life to protect them, and I was never thanked. That didn't use to bother me, but it does now.

But our sire bond isn't like that. The intensity, the devotion to each other, isn't an obligation. I could walk away, and Jasik couldn't stop me. But I don't want to. I feel him inside me on a cellular level. His blood courses through my veins. I am happier when he's around. I feel a calming wave washing over me, and though it's all-consuming, I like the way he makes me feel. I am confident and beautiful, strong and coveted. We truly care for each other, and that's how it should be. He and I are a team, and we fight to stop the rogues once and for all.

I glance over at Jasik and find him staring at me. I feel my cheeks growing hot, the blood pooling there to betray my innermost desires. This is the only bad thing about being so transparent with my emotions. The ones I don't want on display are the strongest and most obvious. Jasik is a bit harder to read, but I'm getting better at it.

"Staring is impolite," I tease.

"I guess I'm a rude man," he says. Every so often, his English accent coats his words in a delectable manner. He's spent so much time in the States, it's almost a treat when I hear it. This same thing happens to Malik and Amicia. Their accents are muddled by their American cadence.

He winks at me, and my knees are weak. His eyes are bright red and glowing. His skin is pale and radiant in the moonlight. Everything about him shimmers. He's the most enchanting person I've ever met—and it only took death to introduce us.

I want to talk about the night we almost kissed, but I don't mention it. He hasn't either. I wonder if he thinks I regret it. Am I not giving off the right signals? I wish I had someone to talk to about boys and love and the right way to kiss someone.

Liv was always my go-to gossip queen. We navigated our emotions with late-night chats, raw cookie dough, and romantic comedies. Now the only person I can talk to is Hikari, but just because she looks my age doesn't mean she is. She's probably closer to one hundred than seventeen. I don't even bother considering Amicia.

The only reason we almost kissed was because my blood lust got the better of me. I never would have tried seducing him if I hadn't drunk his blood. I mean, the middle of an epic fight isn't the best time to take our relationship to the next level. So far, Jasik has been courtly. It's his nature, and I know this. But I think I want more.

I still can't believe I just thought that. There was a time I'd convinced him I had no intention of staying at the manor. I wanted to learn from him and be on my way back to the witches. I'm not sure I ever told him I've changed my mind, that there's no going back for me.

"Jasik, you know I'm happy, right?" I say.

He eyes me curiously, a brow arched in confusion. He's probably thinking that that was a random statement. If only he could follow my thoughts . . .

No! Scratch that. The last thing I need is for him to be *inside* my head.

"I suppose so, yes," he says.

"I just . . . I hope you know I like how things are now."

"What things?"

Something in the distance moves. A twig snaps, and our heads jerk toward the noise. Before I can consider what's happening or how I'm going to answer his question, Jasik moves in front of me, putting himself between the noise and me. After a few seconds, a skunk trudges from a bush. The moment the tiny creature notices us, his ears perk up and tail stands on end. Thankfully, his fluffy black-and-white butt is pointed in the other direction. The last thing I need right now is to be sprayed.

"Come on," I caution, pulling Jasik by the arm. We leave the creature to continue its scavenging.

Several minutes have passed, and I still haven't answered Jasik's question. I know it's too late to respond now, but I can't stop thinking about what he said.

What things?

What things am I happy with now?

If I don't answer him in a totally chill, nonchalant way, he's going to assume I mean I like the way things are between us right now, and that's not true, is it?

I groan internally. Sometimes I hate being an emotional teenager. I can't make up my mind about anything. On top of that indecisive fest, I am daunted by the scattered emotions of a newborn vampire. Heightened senses are fantastic. Heightened emotions aren't so great.

"I just meant I'm happy living with the vampires," I finally say.

Jasik nods. "They're happy you're there."

"Are you?" I whisper.

Jasik stops walking and keeps his gaze straight ahead. I know he's processing my words, and I think I've finally given him the push he needs to make a move—or, at the very least, to *talk* about that night. Our gazes meet, and I swear my heart is impaled by a lightning bolt. It's as if Thor himself is urging me to continue, so I do.

"Ava..." Jasik's voice is soft. I love the way my name dances past his lips.

I step forward, closing the space between us. The wind flutters through the trees, blowing the branches in such a way, it's as if they sing just for our ears tonight.

I rest my palms against his chest and look up at him. His jaw is clenched tightly shut; the tiny muscles in his cheeks shift as his tension eases.

Suddenly the chill is gone and the night is warm, misty, and a haze forms all around us. The air is so moist, it's hard to breathe. I inhale the breaths he exhales, and it's oddly erotic.

I lean closer, and something rustles in the distance. Jasik spins around, finding nothing but darkness. It seems the forest is empty tonight, with nothing but the two of us and my ever-growing restlessness.

Can't a girl catch a break?

My heart is hammering a hundred beats a second. I feel like I'm a child again and I've just been caught sneaking out of my room to play after Mamá has already scolded me for not going to bed as instructed.

Clearly feeling as though we're surrounded by spies, we both ready ourselves for an attack. Except it never comes. Once again, Jasik and I are alone with nothing but our unruly emotions.

"I'm not expecting this to be an eventful hunt," Jasik says quietly. I'm not sure if he's talking to me or trying to calm himself, but I answer him.

"I think we're the only vampires in the woods tonight," I say, hoping to ease his nerves. Jasik seems on edge, and I'm not sure if it's because of something I'm doing or if it's because we're supposed to be patrolling and we're letting our emotions get in the way. It's careless, sloppy work, but I don't care.

"That doesn't seem to bother you anymore," Jasik says as he turns to face me.

His words bring me crashing down. Once on cloud nine, I'm now rooted firmly on earth and back in my head. Almost immediately, my desire to pick up where we left off is extinguished. I cross my arms over my chest, giving the universal signal guys know well. I must come off harsh, because Jasik seems to cower beneath my stare.

I'm certain he can sense my agitation. I hate for him to think I'm on edge because of something he did or said, when really, I'm upset with myself. My sudden anxiety has nothing to do with him and everything to do with the fact that we're right. We're alone in these woods, which means we *still* haven't seen a rogue vampire.

What are the chances that they wouldn't be around two nights in a row? Something is happening. The others may not sense it, but I do. This feels exactly like before, when I sensed danger and no one in my coven believed me. Even though I'm enjoying my new life, I can't help but wonder how different things would be if Mamá had just believed me. No one had to die that night, including me.

"It doesn't make you uncomfortable when the rogues are in hiding?" I ask.

Jasik exhales loudly and shrugs. "No more than when the witches are missing."

"Hikari explained their disappearance. Can you explain the rogues going MIA?" I counter. I hope I don't come off as argumentative, but I'm irritated that no one seems to care about this except me. I may be a novice vampire, but I have my common sense.

Something. Is. Happening.

And I will make Jasik see it too.

"Their sire was killed. That can inflict a lot of damage on a nest," Jasik says.

"So their leader is gone and they're making a run for it? It would be nice to have fewer rogues in Darkhaven," I say a little too excitedly.

"Not exactly. I don't expect them to leave town, but someone will step up to lead them," Jasik explains.

Just terrific. Of course someone will step up, because a moment's peace is just too much to ask. The rise of a new leader can only mean difficult times ahead. My earlier happiness is squashed, and I only have myself to blame. I suppose I can never be too happy while still residing in Darkhaven. It's like it senses it and then crushes it.

"And what does that entail?" I ask. I'm partly readying myself for what's to come, but also, the inner workings of the vampire world are fascinating. I used to think they lived their lives in solitude, but that's not the case at all. This is where the movies are way off.

"It depends on how many step forward," Jasik says. "Only one can lead, so there will be a duel to determine the strongest leader."

"A duel? Like a fight to the death?"

"Exactly. The remaining vampire will be granted temporary leadership over any who wish to stay. Some might leave and try to form their own nest by siring vampires. But not everyone can handle the responsibility."

"What do you mean?" I ask.

"Leaders must take a stand. It's not simply about proving ability. Power and strength are important, especially to rogues. They lost their leader to witches. They will seek retribution for losing their sire," Jasik says.

I freeze. His words loop in my mind over and over again. Jasik is impassive, so I almost trick myself into believing I misheard or misunderstood his words. Have I had a sudden stroke? Am I too hungry to think clearly? This can't possibly be good.

"Does that mean what I think it means?" I ask. I need clarification before I lose my mind.

"That depends on what you think you just heard," Jasik says. He's not often sarcastic, but when he is, he chooses the worst possible moments for comedic relief. He smiles. I don't.

"Are you saying the rogues will attack the witches again?" I ask.

He nods. "This is just how it works, Ava. Losing a sire to our greatest enemy is a big deal. Sires are thought to be formidable opponents, and when one dies, the nest is in a frenzy. Rogues need leadership."

"But they won't be expecting another attack—not this soon! We have to warn them," I say.

"Ava, I know this is hard for you to accept, but they want you out of their lives. You have to stop going there. *They don't want your help.*"

His words sting, but I don't show him how much pain they inflict. I might have accepted that I am destined to live a different life from Mamá, but that doesn't mean it didn't hurt when she turned her back on me . . . *again.*

"I don't care about that. Warning them is the right thing to do. They don't deserve to be slaughtered just because they hate what I am," I argue. "We protect this town from rogue vampires—that doesn't just mean humans."

I don't wait for Jasik to respond. I'm running through the forest, feet smacking the cold, hard ground as I push through the brush. The familiar crunch of frost beneath my soles sends shivers up my spine, but I press on. I'm not far from Mamá's house. I pray I make it before the rogues attack—if they haven't already.

I come to a sudden halt. Already I can hear their screams. Before I can take another step toward them, Jasik grabs on to my arm. His grip is too tight, and it makes my arm ache. His eyes are hard, emotionless.

"Stop, Ava," he says.

I try to pull free, but I can't. He's holding my arm so firmly, his own fingers are turning white.

"Just *think*," Jasik continues.

"There's nothing to think about! The rogues have attacked. The witches need my help!" I'm shouting, and I don't care who hears me.

"They don't want your help!" Jasik growls. This is the

first time I've heard him scream, seen him be this angry with me. "When will you accept that? They don't care about you anymore, Ava. Stop risking your life for someone who would burn you at the stake given the chance."

His words rock me to my core. He's right. If I'd refused to leave the night I transitioned, they would have killed me. They wouldn't have given it a second thought, yet here I am, constantly risking my life, and the lives of those who truly care about me—namely, the vampires—in the name of righteousness.

"You're right," I whisper. His grip on my arm loosens, but he is too smart to fully release me. "I'm sorry."

"I know you want to help them, but we need to be smart about this," Jasik says. "We can't just rush into battle without a plan or backup."

I nod. As much as it kills me to turn away, I must. I barely survived the last fight. If the others hadn't been there, I know I wouldn't have. I need the vampires as much as the witches need me right now.

"But we'll come back with the others?" I ask. "This will be the last time. I swear."

Jasik sighs. "If that's what you really want to do."

"I do. If not for the witches, then to finish this once and for all. No one escapes this time. Tonight, we end this."

✦

I knew it wasn't going to be easy convincing the others to help the witches. After all, every time we've reached out to them, we've risked our own necks. I'm used to the witches' ungratefulness, but the vampires are not. I try to remain empathetic to that while reminding myself they have no emotional attachment to those dying at this very second.

"There's no way you can convince me to go," Hikari says. She speaks firmly, and I know it will take a miracle to convince her.

"Please," I say. It's not much, but it's all I have. I can't force her to go, and I'm pretty sure no one will go if one stays behind. I need all four hunters to agree to help me tonight.

"I'm sorry, Ava, but this is just messed up. After what happened last time... I mean, they didn't even care that we almost died trying to protect them! *You could have died, Ava. We all could have!*" Hikari is shouting now, but I wish she wouldn't.

I know what happened. I understand the depravity of the witches better than anyone in this house, but their innate nature doesn't mean they should die. Deep down, they're just afraid of something they don't understand. They *can* be good people.

"Everyone needs to calm down," Amicia says.

"But this is insane!" Hikari says.

Amicia holds up her hand, immediately silencing the room. The vampires of the house have gathered to witness my inevitable downfall as a member of this nest. They don't speak, but I can feel their eyes boring holes into my body. I wish Amicia had forced them away. I'd feel better if this were more of a one-on-one conversation between the hunters and me.

"Don't think of this as a favor to the witches," I say. My argument is weak, but my intentions are true. I'm not just asking for their help to save the witches. So much more is going on here. If only the hunters would stop and think, they would see this too. This is *our* fight.

"And how should we think of it?" Malik asks. His eyes are emotionless, his tone hard. It pains me to watch him look at me this way. I know he's disappointed in me.

"We need to eliminate the rogues," I say. "Who's to say they stop at the witches? We were all part of the fight that killed their sire. They will come for us next."

"Ava may have a point. She is the one who killed him," Jasik says.

I flash him a smile to thank him for his support.

"Yeah, and you can be objective here, right?" Jeremiah says. "Let's face it . . . Anytime the decision revolves around Ava, you side with her. We can't trust you anymore."

All at once, the hunters quarrel. So many different voices are shouting and defending their choices, it's impossible to hear anyone clearly. It's a jumbled mess and a complete waste of time. My frustration is gnawing away at the pit of my gut and threatening to boil over.

We don't have time for this!

"Everyone *stop*!" I yell. "This is insane. We are wasting time!"

"Ava, when it comes to these witches, you can't think clearly," Malik says. "Far too many times, you have put their well-being before ours, and it must end now."

For once, he does not hide the emotion in his tone. He is not simply angry. He is *hurt*. It takes me several seconds to process this before I can speak.

"Malik is right, Ava. You are not one of them anymore, and if you want to remain a vampire in this house, then you need to choose. *Them or us*," Amicia says, giving me the ultimate ultimatum.

Shocked, I glance around the room. I'm staring into

the eyes of a dozen vampires who rely on the hunters for protection. They are cold, hard, void of emotion. The hunters stare at me with the same disdain. This time, no one will come to my aid. No one will fight to keep me here. I've run out of second chances, and I need to make a choice.

But I can't.

I can't make the choice to stay here if it means condemning innocents to death. The rogues attacked the witches as a trap *for me*. The witches were never part of this. I started it all, and I must end it.

I shake my head and whisper, "Please, don't make me choose." I can feel tears burn behind my eyes, and I pray they won't fall. The last thing I need right now is to prove I am an emotional wreck.

"You must," Amicia says.

"But this isn't about *them*," I argue.

"And this isn't *only* about the rogues," Jasik counters. "Eventually you'll see that you are blinded by your devotion to the witches."

Knowing my sire is siding with the others is like a knife to the heart. It hurts more than I care to admit. I never realized how much he supported me in the past—and how much I really needed that support.

I sniffle and clear my throat before answering. "I know the rogues will come for me, and if that means I must fight beside the witches now to save myself later, then that's what I choose." It kills me on the inside to say this aloud. The last thing I want to do is turn my back on my new family, but they're not giving me another option that I can live with. An eternity is a long time to live with guilt. I just won't do that.

"Ava, don't do this," Jasik says. His voice is a whisper. I

can sense how much my choice to leave hurts him, but I can't ignore what's in my heart.

The house is silent as I turn to leave, and just before I walk out the front door, I say, "Maybe instead of judging me for aiding the very people who gave me my life's blood, you should ask yourselves why it's so easy for you to ignore a fellow supernatural in need. You all talk about ending this feud and living in peace, but in times when you can prove that we are more than monsters, you shy away and leave the witches to be slaughtered. If that is what I must do to live under this roof, then I want no part of it."

ELEVEN

I arrive at Mamá's house in a blaze of glory. At least, I *think* I do. In reality, the fire magic lighting the night sky isn't mine.

Fireballs are carelessly slung through the air, and I dodge one that probably wasn't even aimed for me. At least, I *hope* it wasn't. It would really suck to be killed tonight by the very people I came to help. The last thing I need is to eat crow.

I search the crowd for Mamá, who stops suddenly when she sees me. She's surprised, and her hesitation is exactly what the rogues need. She winces upon impact. The vampire she is fighting strikes her with such ferocity, she is flung backward. Her frail frame lands carelessly atop another few witches who are also fighting to save their lives.

"Mamá!" I scream. I catch the attention of several rogue vampires, who seem just as shocked by my arrival as the witches.

I rush toward her, side-stepping a rogue who lunges at me. I make a mental note to return for him later as I reach Mamá's side.

I help her up, and she leans against me until she stands. This is the closest we've been since my transition. The warmth of her body radiates against my own. It's a scorching heat that burns my skin. I try to ignore the rapid beats of her heart as I aid her, but as each second passes, it gets more and more difficult to separate Mamá from food.

I meet her gaze. Eyes wide with fear, she bleeds from her lip. Instinctively, I glance at her wound, and she sucks in a sharp breath. She pushes me away, and I lose my grip on her. She stumbles into the arms of another witch—someone I don't know.

I don't ask if Mamá is okay—not because I don't care or because this isn't the time. But because if I did ask, she would lie. She wouldn't want to look weak in front of a vampire, even if said vampire is her only child. Her strength used to inspire me. I was awestruck by how easily she handled Papá's death. I was a hellion as a child and even worse as a teenager. It couldn't have been easy to raise me alone.

She winces as the witch supporting her stumbles backward. Instinctively, I reach out to grab Mamá's arm to help steady her, but she whips away from my touch as if I could actually use my magic to burn her. I may unleash agony on rogues, but I would never do that to someone innocent. Her fear stings at my heart. Can't she look into my eyes and see that I'm not evil?

I know Mamá doesn't want me here, and honestly, I don't want to be here. I thought we ended this when I killed their sire, but no, I must fight another day. I wonder if I'll ever retire my stake.

The vampires were right. I can't keep coming here. After tonight, the witches are on their own. With my eyes, I tell Mamá that this is the last time. She doesn't falter. She doesn't care, so I try not to either. After tonight, she'll get her wish. She'll be rid of me forever.

I turn to face the massacre. There are only about a half dozen rogue vampires remaining. Either the rest are dead, or they fled when I arrived. I'm hoping the former. If another rogue from this nest materializes from the shadows, I may actually lose my mind.

"Six rogues," I whisper to myself. "I can handle that. I can do this." I try to mentally prepare myself for fighting on my own. I doubt I can count on the witches to have my back, so I must be smart. No reckless attacks. I don't have the vampires as backup anymore.

I haven't totally processed what that means. I left so abruptly, abandoning my few life treasures to aid the witches and kill more rogues. I must go back for my things, especially for my cross. That's all I have left in the world.

I exhale slowly, calming my nerves and clearing my mind. The rogues are all around me. Some fight with witches; others wait for my attack. I stare into several sets of hungry red irises, and I think I must be a fool to believe I can take on so many rogues at once. Tonight, I need a miracle. I suppose my existence is a phenomenon, so it shouldn't be too much to ask for another.

The grass is stained red with blood. It teases my senses and makes it hard to concentrate. I try to coach myself internally, ignoring my rumbling stomach. There wasn't time for a quick pick-me-up before leaving the manor, and now I'm fighting the urge to lick the ground clean. Fighting alongside mortals is so much harder than it should be. If only they would stop getting injured, I could actually do my job and protect Darkhaven from these fiends.

In the center of the backyard, there is a large tree stump with relics positioned strategically atop. I'm very familiar with this altar and the magical artifacts used to decorate it. Some have fallen to the ground. Others are broken, with shards of glass sticking into the earth like daggers in the gut. The iridescent sphere Mamá uses to represent the moon is still at the center. The full moon is still a couple of weeks away, so I don't understand its purpose in tonight's ritual. What are the witches up to?

Someone screams, distracting me. A rogue vampire is crouched over a witch. She cries out as he pounces atop her, straddling her small frame. I can't see her face, but I sense her fear. She waves her arms frantically before her, scratching at the vampire, desperately trying to free herself. He pins her arms to her side, and her hands spark but the flames quickly extinguish. Her emotions are getting the best of her. Without help, she will die.

This is my chance to prove I came here to help. I must show the witches not all vampires are evil. We do not fight on the side of the rogues. If there will be peace, there must first be war, and I'm okay with that.

It takes less than a second for me to decide to make a spectacle of this kill. The witches must see what vampires are willing to do to bring this feud to an end. We could be powerful allies or formidable opponents. Truly, it is their decision.

I dash to the coven's altar and grasp the small sphere in my hand. I know Mamá has many more just like it, so I can sacrifice one. I also want her to know I noticed the altar and that I know moonstone is used for specific rituals only. My dream warned me someone is coming, and I'd bet everything I own the witches know something about that.

In my hand, the orb glows brightly. The crystal vibrates at my touch, sending shock waves radiating down my arms and straight to my soul. Never before has moonstone affected me so deeply. I gasp as the sensation spreads, setting my entire body aflame. I shake my head and hold it tightly. I don't have time to think about this. Not when I'm surrounded by rogues, and witches are dying.

I toss the shimmery globe in the air, catching it on its downfall, and wait for the perfect moment. I whistle loudly, catching the rogue's attention, and throw the sphere directly at him. He sits upright, jerking his head to the side. The whistle is an ear-piercing screech that even bothers me.

The rogue turns at the perfect moment, and the orb shatters against his head with such brutality, his skull shatters. He bursts into ash, and the witch sits upright. She's shivering, arms wrapped around her torso as she frantically searches for her savior. We make eye contact in seconds.

Liv.

Her eyes are wide when she sees me. Tears stream down her cheeks, and her mouth opens in a soft gasp. I hear it even across the yard. I stand straighter, stronger, and defiantly look her straight in her eyes.

Yes, it's me, the girl you used to be best friends with. I may look different, but I'm the same girl who's saved your life countless times, the same girl you told you never wanted to see for the rest of your life. Maybe if I listened, you'd be dead right now. Think about that!

I turn back toward the rogues and withdraw my stake.

One down. Five to go.

My weapon is far too light in my grasp. My palms are slick from the moisture in the air. I squeeze my hand tighter, careful not to snap my stake into pieces. The last thing I need right now is to be outnumbered *and* completely weaponless.

Witches are battling rogues, but some have already retreated toward the house. I don't worry about them. I've done all I can to prove I'm here to help, and if they're smart, they'll work with me. Now or never, they need to *trust* me.

Fire witches are gathering together, holding hands to strengthen their control over the element. The sudden heatwave is melting the frost that coats the ground and making the air so muggy, it's difficult to breathe. They should use their combined strength to take out a few rogues, but they don't. Instead, they let me do the dirty work. I don't understand why they've suddenly retreated, and there's no time to question their efforts or give orders.

Trying to remain optimistic, I consider the haze advantageous. This will allow me to sneak up on unsuspecting rogues.

It takes no time at all to find one. He's too busy searching the yard for another witch—or for me. I'll never know, because I sink my stake into his back, shoving it so deep I can hear bone snap. He turns to ash before he even knows he's dead.

Two down. Four to go.

I blink through the mist, finding it harder and harder to hunt my prey in this fog. I can't see the witches, but I hear them chanting. No doubt they have all linked arms, forming a circle to summon their elements, leaving me to eliminate the threat on my own. I wish I could be surprised, but I'm used to this. No one helped when I was part of their coven, so why would they help now?

The rash change in temperature is making my skin crawl. The air is hot, moist, and it coats my face. I wipe away the sweat that drips from temple to chin and push back loose strands of frizzy hair.

No longer frozen, the earth is softening. The familiar crunch beneath my feet is gone, and I squish into the wet grass and mushy soil with each step I take. The spongy splash of each step mashes around my brain, and I squirm.

The elements are distracting me from tracking my next victim, and I need to focus. I inhale deeply. The torrid air is sticky in my lungs. I resist the urge to hack. Instead, I clear my throat, and a rogue finds me.

He pounces from beyond the haze. I don't see him until he's already upon me. We tumble to the ground and land in a loud smack. I sink into the earth and feel the mud mash into the crevices of my body.

I'm holding him away from me with one arm and frantically searching for my lost stake with the other. Like a feral hound, the rogue's jaws are snapping at me. Only an inch from my skin, the rogue's saliva seeps from his mouth and slops onto my cheek.

His breath is wretched, his teeth decaying, his lips bloodstained. I feel bile rising in my chest, and I force it down.

My fingers tease something hard, cool. I groan loudly as I stretch my arm too far, but I brush against the metal with enough force to roll it toward me. I sink my fingers into the ground, dirt caking beneath my fingernails, as I wrap the weapon in my palm.

I smack my forehead against the rogue's nose, and he falters. I push him backward, jabbing the heel of my hand forward to strike him in the chest. Angered, he crushes down on me in a huff, but I've already moved my stake to intercept his attack. He combusts atop me, and I stand quickly. His remains blow off my chest with the help of a quick burst of air.

Three down. Three to go.

I'm beginning to appreciate my odds, but I try not to be overjoyed. When I get cocky, things go horribly wrong, and I don't have any allies to rely on. I need to be smart and utilize the elements in my attacks.

I try to trudge softly through the yard, but I can barely see even a few feet in front of me.

I stop abruptly, eying something in the distance. It's a shadow figure that makes my heart melt. I flash to my dream world. Something about being here, in this exact place, makes me queasy. This is too familiar, especially with the witches here.

Slowly, I walk toward the figure. Several feet away, I spot a rogue. She's spinning in circles, turning around so quickly, she doesn't even see me rushing toward her.

I leap into the air, jumping onto her back. I cling to her, wrapping my legs around her waist and arms around her chest. I drive my stake into her chest with a loud grunt. She screams as it makes impact, and we fall to the ground. By the time my knees touch grass, she's gone.

Four down. Two to go.

Still on all fours, I grab my stake. I glance up in time to see someone running at me. She reaches me at the same time I try to stand. Her foot makes impact with my chest, and I fall onto my bottom. She kicks again, and I tumble backward. With one final grunt, she whips her fist at me, and I'm flying through the air.

I crash against the fence, taking part of it down with me. A section spears upright and slices into my back. I cry out as it punctures through the front of my shirt.

The rogue vampire is upon me now, smiling down as she towers over me. I can't move. Even if I try to wiggle free, she will just force me down again. The predator has become the prey, and I've never been so angry in my life. I refuse to believe this is how my life ends.

She walks closer, stepping between my legs. She's confident that I've lost, that she's won. She believes she will be my end, and I take full advantage of this opportunity.

I slap my legs together, hitting her ankles, and she yelps as she falls forward. She tries to break her fall, but her hand lands on another pointed picket. It slices through her hand, and she cries out for help. Somewhere out here, there is another rogue vampire. I need to move quickly before he finds us.

I reach for a picket, snap it free, and thrust my newfound weapon into her spine, completely missing her heart. She gasps as I withdraw it and aim better. She's dead by the time the final rogue vampire reaches us.

He leaps atop me, scrunches my jacket in his hands, and yanks me toward him. It takes but a second to pull my limp body free from the picket that impaled my gut only moments ago, but pain radiates down my legs in rushing waves with no hint of stopping. I cringe, grinding my teeth together, as the rogue vampire pulls me so close to his face, our noses touch.

He spins in a circle and tosses me into the yard. I collide with the witches, who have formed a mini circle near the sliding glass doors. The moment I crash into them, they break their circle, and the elements are freed. The haze dissipates, the air cools, and the ground slowly begins to harden once again.

The air is clear, and the rogue vampire smiles as he makes his way toward me.

"You guys can chip in any time now," I grumble as I struggle to stand. My legs ache, and my knees buckle when I put weight on them.

With the picket withdrawn, I'm beginning to heal, but I still feel the pain. With each step, the gaping wound in my gut screams at me to stop, to rest, to feed, but I cannot.

I run toward the rogue, fumbling forward clumsily. Immediately, I know something is wrong. My legs feel heavy, the weight of them cumbersome.

We're both playing a desperate game of chicken that really no one can win. When we reach each other, I lash out at him, but I miss. He doesn't. He makes contact with me not once, not twice, but three times. He slams his fist into my chest, and ribs snap.

I inhale sharply, and my lungs protest. I want to scream at the witches, but I don't. It's no use. They don't care that I'm here, and they have no intention of aiding me. As far as they're concerned, if I die, there will be one less vampire in Darkhaven.

Tonight, I must fight alone.

"I'm really getting tired of you," the rogue hisses into my ear. He grabs me by the neck and slams my body to the ground. The earth craters around my frame. Already weakened by my earlier assault, my spine snaps, and I can't feel my legs. I try to move them to no avail. Panic sets in, but I push it down.

The vampire smiles. He releases my neck and straddles my torso.

"This really doesn't look good, Ava," he taunts.

He grabs my chin with his cold, bony fingers.

I can still move my arms, so I scratch at his hands. He laughs at me and forces my head to the side. He whips my neck too quickly and pushes too hard, stretching my muscles farther than they can go. I hear the distinct tear of flesh giving way, and it echoes in the air. I cry out and stop struggling.

"Look at them," he says, seething. "It wasn't supposed to happen this way. *They* were supposed to be the present for *you*."

My vision is cloudy, and I blink to clear it. The rogue's breath is hot on my cheek. He licks my tears, starting at my chin and making his way to my eye. I choke on my breath, gagging at being so close to such a disgusting creature.

"You weren't supposed to be here," he says in a singsong voice. He *tsks* me playfully. "This was your surprise and my reckoning." He smiles, and his eyes are lifeless, soulless, showcasing the true monster within him.

Jasik was right. Someone did step forward to lead the rogues, and that very vampire is atop me now.

I consider stalling him. With each passing second, my bones harden, my flesh tethers together, and I am revitalized. I succeed in wiggling my toes, but it takes all my effort to move them. *I need more time.*

"Where are your friends?" the rogue asks. He sits back, resting his butt on my pelvis. I groan as he applies too much pressure to my spine, but he is unaffected by my protest.

He scans the vacant woods, searching for the vampires. Of course, I know they are not there, but he doesn't. If he looks long enough, I'll be healed enough to move again.

My mind wanders to the magic Holland and I used the other day. It was powerful, and it's always nestled inside me. In battle, I rely too much on my vampire abilities. Perhaps it's time the witch within me saves the day.

I search for it, finding it growing stronger. It's bubbling over, revitalizing my wounds and strengthening each break, each tear, each weakness. It takes only seconds, but already, I feel better, healthier, and even stronger than before.

I roll my ankles while the vampire is still staring into the distance. He continues to taunt me.

"I don't see them," he sings. He's overjoyed, believing to

be witnessing both my abandonment and downfall.

I sit upright, startling him. He tries to fall back, to put some space between us, but sitting on his own legs, he's trapped himself. This time, I smile, offering a wicked grin that hopefully resembles something sinister.

I grab him by the throat, squeezing as hard as I can. He chokes, gasping for air.

"That's because I don't need them to save me," I say behind a clenched jaw.

I see myself in his eyes, and something flashes there. It's a bright light, and it engulfs him completely. He screams as he's lit aflame, consumed by the fire in my soul. After only a few blinks, he's gone. His ashes are blowing away in the breeze, and I'm standing, dusting off my chest. My legs are still weak, but I'm growing stronger with each breath I take. The more I succumb to the magic inside me, the better I feel.

With the rogue vampires gone, I stare at the witches. I wait for someone to speak. Maybe they'll thank me. Maybe they'll finally see that I have no intention of hurting them so long as they don't come after me. The seconds tick by as we stare at each other in silence.

"*Te dijeron que nunca volvieras*," Mamá says. "Why did you come back? *Para mi?*"

I shake my head, sadly unsurprised by my mother's lack of emotion. "No, I didn't come back for you. I came to stop them."

"And you did, so just go," Liv says. She's standing beside Mamá, where I would be if the situation were different. I know I'll never stand there again, and I'm starting to be okay with that. I used to believe vampires were the monsters under my bed, but now I see the truth. Witches tell their youth stories about evil and darkness and beasts that look like humans, but in reality, *they* are the monsters.

Without another word, I leave. I don't look back. I don't cry. I don't even care that they're too stubborn to realize I would have been a real asset, a true guardian of Darkhaven.

Aiding the witches to eliminate a shared enemy was the right thing to do, so I don't regret coming here, even if that means I've lost my new family.

I limp into the forest when I sense them. They're rushing toward me and at my side before I even realize what's happening. I lean against a tree and sigh. Smiling, my heart explodes in my chest. A sob escapes my lips, and I push myself from the tree to walk toward them.

"You came," I whisper.

My vampires, my allies, my friends, my family . . . All four stand before me now. Jasik is at my side and pulls me into his arms. He hugs me, squeezing his arms so tightly, I screech. I can feel his concern, his love, and his pain for letting me go without him.

He holds my head in his hands and stares into my eyes. He doesn't speak because he doesn't need to. I can read his emotions in his eyes. He's happy I'm alive, annoyed that I left, and grateful it's finally over.

I hope he can read mine too. He needs to know I don't harbor resentment toward him or any of the others. Fighting alone is something I needed to do. I learned something invaluable tonight. I discovered I rely too much on the vampires, and I don't need to. There's a ruthless magic inside me, and I can use it to protect myself.

"Everything okay?" Hikari asks.

I pull away from my sire to face the others. Nodding, I say, "It's finally over."

"You're sure no one escaped?" Jeremiah asks. He scans the woods, finding nothing but dead brush and the subtle shimmer of frost coating the earth.

I shrug. "I don't know, but it's over for me."

I lean against Jasik, and Malik walks over.

"I'm surprised you came," I say to my trainer.

He smiles at me. "You were pretty convincing tonight."

I nod. "I was right, you know, even if it didn't work out as I planned."

Malik arches a brow. "What do you mean?"

"I was hoping they would finally see that we're not evil, but they didn't care that I came. They even left me to fight the rogues by myself."

Jasik tenses beside me. I know he's angry with them, but he doesn't want to fight with me about this. Not again. Not tonight. Maybe tomorrow we'll have a long talk about what this means for us, for Darkhaven. This town has always been my home, but I wonder if it's becoming too dangerous to stay. Everywhere we go, we'll have to watch ourselves. The witches can attack at any moment, and now I truly believe they will. That dream was a warning, and I won't forfeit this advantage.

"I know you want peace, but we've been vampires a lot longer than you, Ava. This isn't the first time someone with such a pure heart has turned and wanted to create a better future," Jasik says.

I glance over my shoulder. I can see light at Mamá's house through the trees, but I don't see the witches. And I don't care to. I tried. For far too long, I protected them, defended them, and in return, I've only suffered from their abuse. Not anymore. My conscience is clear, and I can walk away from my past with no regrets.

As we slowly trudge home, I think about the last thing Mamá said to me. She asked why I was there, and she reminded me I wasn't supposed to come back.

This time, I'll listen.

Next time, I won't return.

TWELVE

When I wake, I'm stiff. My eyes are tired. I look around the room, my gaze landing on the vampire sleeping beside me.

I'm back in my bedroom at Amicia's manor. Fully clothed, Jasik snores softly. He's lying on his back, chiseled features hard as the ceiling fan swooshes his tousled hair. He frowns, his brow furrowing, and I wonder what he's dreaming about. Where does he go when he closes his eyes?

I reach for him but stop short of brushing my fingers against his skin. I don't want to wake him.

I sit up and try to shimmy off the bed. The floor is scattered with empty blood bags. My stomach grumbles when I see them. I remember feeding last night, but Jasik must have stayed to help me. The night is a bit of a blur.

By the time we made it home, I was exhausted, starving, and losing strength far too quickly. My body was healing, but I needed to refuel. I remember Jasik carrying me upstairs, and later, I remember him waking me to drink. Everything else is foggy.

I scratch my head, and my fingers get tangled in my hair. Tiptoeing into the bathroom, I assess the damage in the mirror. Aside from a wicked case of bedhead and the layer of dried mud coating most of my body, no one would ever know I left the manor last night. My wounds have healed, and I'm actually feeling pretty good.

After I shower, I dress quickly, leaving my discarded dirty clothes in a heap on the tile floor. Quietly, I open the door, hoping not to wake Jasik. I have every intention of finding Amicia, thanking her for agreeing to send the vampires, and apologizing for my behavior. They were right: I was blinded by the witches, and even though I had every intention of stopping the rogues, I wasn't completely honest about my motivations. I did want to protect my coven. It's all I've ever known.

"Sneaking out?"

Jasik's voice is husky with sleep, a slow rasp that is strangely arousing. I've never seen him the exact moment he wakes. I've never been the first person he's seen either. Thankfully, I don't look like the hot mess I woke up as. I'm clean, dressed in fresh clothes, and my hair is braided in one long thread down my back.

I face him, feeling my cheeks heat at the sight of him. He's sitting up in bed, back resting against the headboard. He'd changed since last night. He's wearing a loose-fitting T-shirt that hangs raggedly off one shoulder, and I can see the top of his defined torso. His jogger pants emphasize his solid legs, which are perched atop my bed, feet linked at his ankles.

He smiles at me, eyes tired, hair ruffled, and I realize just how deep into this budding relationship I truly am. There's something breathtaking about this man, and there's something inside me that wants him to discover the untouched curves of my body. I crave him in ways I've never experienced.

I swallow hard and walk toward him. My legs are heavy, the space between us intimate.

"Good morning," I say softly. My voice squeaks, and I curse internally. How is Jasik so much better at controlling his emotions, his desires?

He chuckles. "Good morning, Ava."

When he says my name, I just about die on the inside. There's something about my name on his lips with his accent that sets me on fire. I bite my lower lip, and he watches me. His jaw clenches shut, and his heart races.

A hard knock at my bedroom door reminds me we're not alone. I glance at Jasik curiously, but he shrugs. Apparently he wasn't expecting a visitor either.

"Come in," I say loudly, and the door opens.

Malik enters, face unreadable. My heart sinks when I see him. This look means one of two things: either he's still upset with me or he's about to ruin what was the start of a wicked good day. I cross my arms over my chest, as if I can shield myself from the damage about to occur. Can I just go back in time and lock the door?

"We have a situation," Malik says.

Jasik tosses his legs over the side of bed and strides toward him. His feet are bare, and the hardwood floor squeaks under his weight.

"What happened?" I ask.

He need not respond. I already know the answer. There is only one person who can ruin my day. I made my peace with her last night, but that never seems to be enough.

They say they want me out of their lives, but how can I walk away if she keeps pushing us together?

"The witches are outside," Malik says.

It feels like every single tiny hair on my body stands on end. My senses are acutely aware of everyone in the room. I hear Jasik's breath hitch and Malik's disgruntled tone. I hear my heartbeat race to brain-tingling levels, and I feel my insides twist.

Can there never be peace?

"They're *here*?" I ask.

"They want to speak with you, Ava," Malik says, confirming my question.

This catches my attention. "Wait—You *talked* to them? You went outside?" I ask.

Malik nods. "Someone had to. They knocked on the door and shouted that they weren't leaving until someone answered."

I frown. "How did they know where to find us?"

"What do you mean?" Jasik asks.

"How did they know where we live?" I say, shaking my head. "I never knew this place existed until you brought me here, so how did they find us in one night? I spent years patrolling these woods, and I never found this place. There's no way they could without help."

"Maybe they used magic?" Jasik offers.

I did consider this. If they had something or someone to search for, they could try a locater spell, but they would need something to connect where they are with who they seek, like a link. To find me, they couldn't just connect to my magic; they would need something of mine to find me. And they couldn't use just any item. It would need to be something spectacularly special—something I covet.

My heart sinks.

"My stake!"

I rush around the room, frantically searching for the clothes I discarded after I showered. I find them in a bundle on the floor, but my jacket isn't there.

"Where is my jacket?" I shout as I tear through the pile of dirty clothes. Maybe if I keep looking, it will magically appear.

Jasik dashes to my makeup table, where he must have left my jacket last night. In a flash, he's back, handing the garment to me. "Here."

I search the pockets, but I don't find it. My heart stops.

"No," I whisper. "It's *gone*."

"What do you mean?" Malik asks.

"I must have dropped it in the fight."

I'm shaking. I ball my hands into fists and scratch at my palms, hoping to steady my breathing. I can't think. I can't focus. My mind is foggy, my brain heavy in my head. The room is closing in on me, and I can't breathe.

"You think the witches have it?" Malik asks.

I nod, grinding my teeth. "I think they used it to find me."

"Maybe they'll give it back," Jasik says.

I want to be hopeful, but Mamá knows how much this stake means to me. It's one of two items I have of Papá's, and now that she hates what I've become, I think she would keep my stake from me out of spite.

I bet she has it on her. It will be strapped to her thigh. She'll want me to see it, to know she has it and used it to take away our peace of mind. The witches know where we live, and now they have the upper hand. At any point, they can visit us when the sun is high in the sky, and they can use their magic to spark a flame that sends us all straight to hell.

"I hope so," I whisper. My hands are white-knuckled fists, holding my jacket to my chest as I try to steady my racing heart. "It was my father's."

Jasik rubs his hand up and down the length of my back, cooing me into relaxation. I lean against him, resting my head against his arm. Just when I thought the witches were out of my life for good, they're back, and I'm missing the only thing from Papá I can actually touch.

I toss my jacket on my bed as I open the drawer to my bedside table. The small black jewelry box is still tucked safely inside. I pick it up and run my finger along the edge. This is all I have left of him now. I take a deep breath and touch the silver cross.

The vampires watching tense. I hear their breath catch as I run my fingertip down the length of the cold metal. I wait for something to happen. Anything at all. But nothing does. I grab on to the cross and pull it free from the box. The box falls to the ground in an echoing heap that tears through the silent room. The cross rests in the palm of my hand, and I spin to face the others.

The brothers are staring, jaws slack, eyes wide. Their shock is evident. I hold out my hand, unable to speak, showing them the cross. I walk toward them, and both scurry back until their backs are flush against the wall. I stop before I touch them.

"H-How?" I stutter.

"That's not possible," Malik whispers.

Jasik steps forward and reaches for my hand. Time seems to slow as he moves closer and closer. His fingers are long and slender, pale and cold. His hand shakes as he tries to steady himself for impact.

Malik grabs his brother's hand before we make contact. He moves so quickly, I flinch.

"Don't!" Malik shouts.

Jasik shakes free and quickly rushes forward. The moment his skin graces the cross, it sizzles. He shrieks, an earth-shattering scream that pierces my heart. His hand is set aflame, and he yanks his arm back to extinguish the fire. He cradles his wounded arm against his body and rocks back and forth.

I wait for his skin to heal, but it doesn't.

"What's happening? Why aren't you healing?" I ask. I look at his brother to Jasik's wound and back again.

"It takes a lot longer to heal this type of wound," Jasik says. He grinds his teeth when he talks and groans at the pain my cross caused. I never realized one simple religious symbol held so much power over the undead.

Malik disappears into my bathroom and returns with bandages. He wraps his brother's wound quickly, applying enough pressure to stop the bleeding.

"I warned you," Malik chastises.

"I needed to see," Jasik explains.

Malik shakes his head and mumbles under his breath before turning to face me.

"These wounds are more painful and take longer to heal," Malik explains. "This is why that was a stupid idea."

"But I can touch it," I say softly. I clasp my hand, relishing in the feeling of the cross against my skin. I haven't touched this treasure since I turned, and it's killed me to feel so disconnected from Papá. Every time I thought of him and how detached I felt from my heritage, I died a little on the inside.

I fumble to unlatch the chain before securing it to my neck. The metal is shiny and bright, and it feels cool against my skin. I keep my hand on it, unable to stop myself from making sure it's still there. I can feel it against my skin, and it hums. I close my eyes and let that feeling wash over me.

"I can't believe this is happening," I whisper. I want to scream, to cry, to shout. I've never felt so happy, so beloved, so enthralled with any one object in all my life, but this cross means more to me than I could ever explain to the vampires. To them, it's a symbol of death, and it's the main reason the witches have a hard time seeing vampires as good, pure beings.

"It appears you have a few more tricks up your sleeve," Jasik says, trying to keep the mood light.

I smile at his words, excitement bubbling within me. "I wonder what else I can do."

✦

I open the door and step onto the front porch. Per my request, the vampires have agreed to stay inside the manor, but I know they're waiting in the foyer for this meeting to inevitably go wrong.

Before I stepped outside, the vampires told me what would happen if the witches attacked. There would be no backing down. They know where we live now, and they brought the fight to our doorstep. The hunters must protect their nest. Doing so means the witches will fall.

Once again, Amicia gave me a choice: us or them. I chose the vampires without hesitation.

Now, I'm staring at my former coven, and I can't help but feel powerful. They seem small, frail, and feeble. I strut toward them, instinctively patting the gargoyle on the head as I take the steps down to the front walk.

"What are you doing here?" I ask as I approach the witches.

"Did you think you were the only one who could show up uninvited?" someone asks.

I glance at her, my irritation growing. I recognize her immediately as Liv's mother. Her brown hair is erratic with tight curls. Her skin is pale, but not as pale as mine. Her long, flowy pants flicker in the breeze, and her eyes are light brown. I notice the dark circles under her eyes almost immediately. I'm happy to know I'm not the only one losing sleep these days.

I've met her a total of two times. After my last visit, Liv told me I wasn't allowed to come over anymore. Her mother didn't agree with our ways. She was a free-loving flower child, and she didn't believe in violence. To spend time together, Liv would sneak out at night to patrol with me. When she slept over, she told her mother she was staying somewhere else.

"Why are you here?" I say, looking directly at Mamá. My gaze settles on her hips. My stake is not there. When I meet her gaze again, she is smiling. She knows I know how she found me, but what she doesn't realize is how close she is to the edge. She will return what belongs to me, even if I have to take it by force.

"*Relájate, niña,*" Mamá says.

Relax? She can't be serious. Our greatest enemies just showed up on our front lawn, and they don't exactly have a history of being helpful or wanting peace. Them showing up here can only mean one thing, and it won't be good.

"We need your help," Liv's mother says.

I gawk at them.

"Are you kidding me?" I blurt. My tone betrays how laughable I find this. For *months*, I've done nothing but try to help them. Time and time again, I risked my life to save theirs. My friends even joined me to help them, and they've been nothing but dismissive.

"We know this is—"

"Unbelievable?" I interrupt.

"Ava," Mamá says. Her tone is cold, sharp, and it makes me feel like a child again. I'm no longer the strong, powerful woman I was just a second ago. I'm weak, vulnerable, and desperately seeking my mother's approval. I hate her for making me feel this way.

"We can't find her alone," the witch whispers. Only then do I see the tears blurring her vision. She lets them flow freely, not brushing them away or hiding her weakness.

"Find who?" I ask. "What happened?"

"A witch is missing," Mamá says.

I shake my head. "No, the rogue explained that was just a trick, a setup to get us all together. He lied. He didn't take anyone."

"*No, mija,*" Mamá says. "Someone has been taken."

"When? Who? How did this happen?" My thoughts are spiraling out of control, and I can sense the witches aren't telling me everything. I'm tired of their lies. I was supposed to be free of them and this burden, but here they are, finally seeking *my* help. I'm not sure how I feel about this. So badly, I want to scream that I'm not falling for this again, but instead, I remain silent, waiting for her response.

"We haven't seen her since last night," Mamá says.

"Who? Who is missing?" I shout.

I'm annoyed and frustrated that the witches still aren't telling me everything. I don't understand what's going on. How could someone be missing? We killed the rogues. I refuse to believe one escaped just to return yet again and rehash a failed plan.

"*Who is missing?*" I ask again.

"Liv."

ALSO BY DANIELLE ROSE

DARKHAVEN SAGA

Dark Secret

Dark Magic

Dark Promise

Dark Spell

Dark Curse

PIECES OF ME DUET

Lies We Keep

Truth We Bear

**For a full list of Danielle's other titles,
visit her at DRoseAuthor.com**

ACKNOWLEDGMENTS

Writing is a team sport, and this career wouldn't be possible without the tireless efforts of a select few.

To Heather, Robin, and Shawna—you three are what keeps me sane. Publishing isn't easy, but having a trio of strong women to confide in helps make it fun. I wouldn't be where I am in my career without your support, talent, and wisdom. I appreciate you all.

To my momma—I really hit the family lottery when I got you. You are fearless in your shameless promotion of my books (even when the cashier at the gas station really doesn't care to hear about my job). I love you.

To my readers—I *literally* couldn't do this job without you. A writer is nothing without a reader, and I never forget that. I am a full-time author because of you, and I am eternally grateful. From the bottom of my heart, *thank you*. Your support and excitement never go unnoticed.

To my Waterhouse Press family—I never imagined my life could be this exciting. I owe so much to you, and not a day goes by when I don't feel immensely grateful and incredibly honored to be part of this family.

ABOUT DANIELLE ROSE

Dubbed a "triple threat" by readers, Danielle Rose dabbles in many genres, including urban fantasy, suspense, and romance. The *USA Today* bestselling author holds a master of fine arts in creative writing from the University of Southern Maine.

Danielle is a self-professed sufferer of 'philes and an Oxford comma enthusiast. She prefers solitude to crowds, animals to people, four seasons to hellfire, nature to cities, and traveling as often as she breathes.

Visit her at DRoseAuthor.com

CONTINUE READING
THE DARKHAVEN SAGA

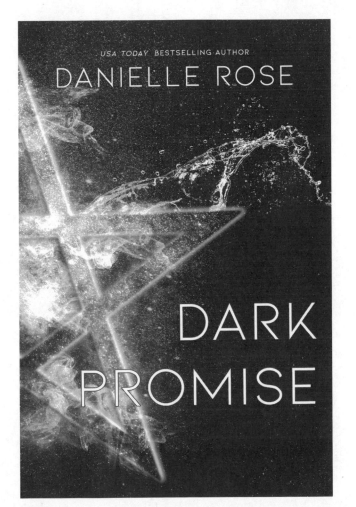